Sunshine State EMP Blackout

Family Reunion

BLOOD IS THICKER SERIES: BOOK ONE

St. Augustine

Punta Gorda

Miami

BRUNO BRENNAN

Sunshine State EMP Blackout

Family Reunion

BLOOD IS THICKER SERIES: BOOK ONE

BRUNO BRENNAN

SIGN UP FOR MY NEWSLETTER

Be the first to know about new book releases, see behind the scenes content and more.

BrunoBrennan.com

For my family, who despite each of our differnces or disagreements, I know we will always be there for one another because
"Blood is Thicker than Water"

SUNSHINE STATE EMP BLACKOUT: FAMILY REUNION
BLOOD IS THICKER SERIES: BOOK ONE

PREFACE

"In an instant, all of the lights go out. Phones, computers, everything electronic, useless. The unthinkable has happened."

Just think about it, no lights, no microwave ovens, no cell phones, only a few working vehicles, no more access to life saving prescription drugs, the grocery shelves bare after mere hours into the event, looting, desperation and nowhere to turn. The government won't be coming to help, they are in the same desperate position. Government officials will be looking to protect and fend for their own families, that includes members of the military and police forces. It will be dog eat dog and only the strongest will survive. Those unprepared don't stand much of a chance in this new reality.

It's no wonder that according to a recent report,

a high-altitude electromagnetic pulse (EMP) could potentially wipe out 90% of the U.S. population within a year due to the crippling of critical infrastructure.

What if in an instant, modern life as we know it was reduced to basic survival? What lengths would you go to protect yourself and your loved ones?

That is what this book endeavors to delve into.

Thank you sincerely for giving me the chance to entertain you and hopefully give you some insight as to what the world might look like in the event of the worst happening and we were actually hit with an EMP. That event could not only come in the form of an intentional attack by terrorists or a foreign government but also by a "Coronal Mass Ejection". Basically, a solar flare that is so big that it devastates things here on earth.

If you think it can't happen, think again, because it already has. In September of 1859 a massive coronal mass ejection (CME) hit Earth's magnetosphere. It is known as the Carrington Event. Named after the British astronomer Richard Carrington, who observed the solar flare that caused the CME.

It was the first documented geomagnetic storm, as it caused auroras to be seen around the world along with widespread telegraph communications failures.

Telegraph wires across North America and Europe failed.

It is considered the most powerful geomagnetic storm ever recorded, estimated to be over 10 times more powerful than any CME in modern history.

If an event of that magnitude occurred today, it would cause catastrophic damage to electronic infrastructure like the electric grid, satellites, GPS systems, and the internet.

Some experts estimate a Carrington-level event today could lead to trillions of dollars in damage globally and take years to recover from.

On average, only about two to three major CME events occur per solar cycle, which is approximately 11 years.

Other significant CMEs occurred in 1921 and 1989, both of which caused power outages and telecommunication issues.

In July 2012, a major CME barely missed the Earth. If it had struck, it could have matched the Carrington Event in strength.

Most experts estimate the likelihood of another Carrington-level event occurring in the next decade to be only around ten to twenty percent.

So, while truly massive and potentially society-crippling CMEs are rare, they are almost inevitable in the long run. The Sun's natural cycles and randomness makes the timing unpredictable.

Not that I actually, sit and worry about such an unlikely event, I do believe being prepared and informed is the best policy.

I'm older now, 59 to be exact, and I live in Miami, Florida. Strangely the same age and location as the main character in this book. My son is recently back from his military duty in the Army, again strangely familiar to one of the characters in this book. My daughter, son-in-law and granddaughter live in Saint Augustine, Florida. I'm sensing a pattern here. My life compared to the chapters that follow.

Ok, I confess that while the book is not autobiographical, it is based on my thoughts as to a plan for my family in the event of some major catastrophe.

Don't be confused, this is most definitely a work of fiction to be sure, but I have over the years thought about what I would do if everything suddenly went dark. Years ago, my family was all together, but as time goes by and life happens circumstances change. So, over the years my thoughts on the matter have had to change and adapt as well.

The characters contained within are not exactly

true to my family members in every aspect, but the general attitudes and tendencies are pretty much spot on. Especially my daughter, as much as she would hate to read this, she is just like her old man, a sarcastic, cynical smart ass through and through. Her husband is for the most part a quiet guy that is very dedicated to his family and especially loving to his daughter. I think even though he is quite reserved on the outside, my belief is that he would storm the gates of Hell to keep his daughter safe. My mother, in this book is a very tough Ol' broad and in many ways, she is in real life as well. She will do whatever needs to be done, but she will piss and moan about it all the while. My son is also a chip off the old block, he has his smartass side as well, but also a very gentle nature that I think serves him well and comforts all those around him. He also has that attitude of family first. Hence the title of this series, "Blood is Thicker."

As far as the scenes where my ex-wife are concerned, well that was just pure therapy for me. She is indeed a very strong woman, I'll give her that, but I did have some fun with her character. Please don't be offended and please forgive me. I'm sure many of the guys reading this book, who have ex-wives will surely understand.

I am a true fan of this genre and I hope I do it justice. One thing that always bothers me about many of the books that I have read in this genre is that no matter what, it always seems the hero of the story and the supporting main characters facing certain doom or misfortune are always bailed out at the last minute by some stroke of fortune. I enjoy that, but sometimes find it a bit incredible. In my tale, some of the characters, including some of the main characters, find themselves in situations that they are unable to escape from without some consequences. While some situations may be disturbing, I've tried to make everything as realistic as possible. Sometimes, the lesser of two evils is the best course of action. So, this book may be a bit harsher in some situations than other books of the genre, but I tried to keep things as realistic as possible. There are no miracles to come in and save the hero at the last minute here. Sometimes reality can be ugly.

Finally, to the character of Maria. I am single and have been pretty much since my marriage fell apart many years ago. It is true, I have had a few relationships since then, but nothing that has lasted the test of time. So, I wrote in a romantic interest for my character. What can I say, I'm a romantic at heart, I truly am. I must say, Maria, if you are out there, please find me soon. I would hate to wait until the apocalypse to find true love.

With all that being said, I hope you enjoy what is to follow. Please remember I am not a professional writer, and my style is somewhat rough I'm sure, but I hope I'm able to entertain you for at least a few hours and hopefully get you thinking about your own family and your own situation if the worst should happen. Please be prepared, because you just never know what the future holds.

Thank you once again and I wish you all the best.
Bruno Brennan

INTRODUCTION

The threat of an electromagnetic pulse (EMP) attack has long concerned security experts and doomsday preppers alike. An EMP is a burst of electromagnetic radiation, caused by an explosion or fluctuation in the atmosphere, that can disrupt and fry electronic devices across a wide area. A powerful enough EMP could knock out entire power grids and render most modern technology useless in an instant.

While the causes of an EMP vary, one of the most feared scenarios is a high-altitude nuclear detonation. The EMP released by such an explosion could blanket entire regions, instantly overloading electrical systems ranging from smartphones to cars to hospital equipment. Aircraft might even fall from the sky. Without electricity, our society would be thrust back into the dark ages, leading to chaos and mass casualties.

However, not all technology would be affected.

Most electronics developed before the widespread adoption of transistor circuitry in the 1960s, such as classic cars, old radios and simple generators, would likely survive an EMP blast intact. Protecting more sensitive devices by enclosing them in Faraday cages can also shield against EMP damage. Those who understand these loopholes, and take proper precautions, stand the best chance of weathering an EMP catastrophe.

This book follows the story of one Florida family determined to survive after a mysterious EMP disables the country's power grid, plunging their lives into chaos. Led by fiercely protective patriarch Joe Kelly, they must rely on grit, supplies Joe has secretly stockpiled, and older modes of transportation to escape the urban anarchy. Their destination is Joe's secluded cabin up north, but reaching it will require ingenuity, courage and sacrifice. This gripping tale explores how far one family will go to stay alive and united in the face of societal collapse and desperate brutality from their fellow man.

TABLE OF CONTENTS

TABLE OF CONTENTS

TABLE OF CONTENTS

CHAPTER ONE
THE STORM BREWS

T he early morning Florida sun beat down on the back patio where Joe Kelly sat cleaning his rifle collection. He worked methodically, taking each gun apart, oiling the mechanisms, and reassembling with an expertise honed over decades of ownership. Joe's salt and pepper hair was neatly trimmed, and his blue jeans and cotton T-shirt were speckled with gun oil. At 59, he still had the solid frame of a man who worked with his hands.

As he finished reassembling a shotgun, Joe clicked on the small radio sitting on the patio table. The voices of talk radio hosts debating politics filled the air. Joe grunted in disgust as he listened to their discussions about new legislation aimed at increasing background checks for firearm purchases.

"More government overreach," Joe grumbled to himself as he started breaking down a hunting rifle.

"Just chipping away at our personal liberties bit by bit."

Inside the house, Joe's son Jojo sat on the living room couch, his eyes fixed on the television as cable news pundits argued loudly. At thirty-three, Jojo still had the close-cropped military haircut he had worn during his years of service in the Army. His brow was furrowed in concern beneath the faded tan beret he wore tilted back on his head.

On the screen, the news ticker flashed increasing global tensions between China, Russia and the United States. Jojo felt his chest tighten anxiously. After serving tours overseas, he was well-versed in the realities of war. The idea of conflict reaching America filled him with dread.

In the kitchen, Joe's daughter Taylor and her husband Jake sat at the table keeping an eye on their 2-year-old daughter, Parker. The curly-haired toddler giggled happily as she ate peanut butter and jelly sandwiches. Jake made silly faces at Parker, eliciting high-pitched squeals of delight.

Taylor smiled at her husband's antics. At thirty, Taylor still resembled the headstrong teenager who used to butt heads with Joe. Her long brown hair tumbled down to her waist in waves and her hazel eyes glinted with intelligence. Beside Taylor sat

Joe's 80-year-old mother, Toni. The elderly woman watched Parker indulgently, her silver hair cut in a curly pixie style.

Joe stepped into the kitchen carrying his cleaning supplies. He raised an eyebrow at Jake playing peek-a-boo with Parker.

"Don't get her too riled up before her nap," Joe said in his gravelly baritone. Jake nodded amiably.

"Wouldn't dream of it, Joe," he replied. Despite Jake's quiet demeanor, Joe knew the young man was devoted to Joe's daughter and granddaughter.

At dinner that evening, the family sat around the table enjoying the pot roast Toni had prepared. As usual, Joe dominated the conversation.

"Did you all hear the Secretary of Defense on the news today?" Joe asked between bites. "Going on about rival nations expanding their EMP technology?"

Taylor sighed, detecting another political rant building. But Jojo looked thoughtful.

"Yeah, sounds like the threat is growing," he replied. "One strategic strike could wipe out the whole power grid. Millions would die in the first year from starvation and disease."

Joe pointed his fork at Jojo. "Exactly. But are our politicians focused on that? No, they're busy ramming more gun control down law-abiding citizens' throats."

Taylor rolled her eyes as she cut up Parker's food. "Oh, c'mon Dad, you always think the sky is falling. I'm sure the government has contingencies in place."

Jake caught Joe's eye sympathetically and gave a slight nod. He didn't engage in these debates, but Joe knew his son-in-law understood his concerns.

After dinner, Joe retreated to his study. He switched on the single overhead bulb and the small space filled with light. Maps covered the walls showing Florida highways, backroads, waterways and topography. Joe selected a well-worn map and unrolled it on his desk.

Tracing his finger along the roads leading out of Miami, he tried to map the likeliest escape routes north towards the rural county where his cabin was located. He was so focused; he didn't notice Jojo enter the room.

"If the cities descend into chaos, the main highways will get jammed quickly," Jojo said.

Joe nodded without looking up. "I figure we'd take twenty-seven up through the state's interior. Avoid the I-95 mess."

"That could work, but there's still a risk of traffic

jams without alternate routes planned," Jojo said. "May I?"

Joe passed his son the map. Jojo studied it, then began plotting less populated backroads running parallel to Highway twenty-seven.

"We can use these to bypass congestion if needed," Jojo said, marking the map decisively.

"Good thinking," Joe said gruffly. He felt better knowing his son's military expertise could aid their escape from the city.

"And dad I have a pretty strong feeling we may be using these routes on foot if we get hit with an EMP, those fancy cars in the driveway are gonna be toast" Jojo said solemnly.

Joe replied "Son, I fear you are one hundred percent correct, and there ain't much cover on US twenty-seven, it's just one long stretch of road with nothing but swamp on both sides. That part of the trip could be very interesting."

CHAPTER TWO
TIME TO GO

The morning sun streamed in through the windows of Joe's Miami home, promising another hot and humid Florida day. Inside, Taylor and Jake were hurrying to finish packing up their SUV for the long drive back to their home in St. Augustine.

Little Parker giggled happily as Jake strapped her into her car seat, planting a kiss on top of her curly head when she was secured. "Ready to hit the road, goofball?" he asked, tickling her belly. Parker erupted in high-pitched squeals of delight.

Taylor smiled indulgently as she watched Jake and their daughter. Her long brown waves were pulled back in a practical ponytail and her sleeveless blouse and shorts were wrinkled from a week of casual vacation wear. She did a final sweep of the living room, checking for any stray toys or belongings.

In the kitchen, Joe was pouring himself a third cup of coffee. Seeing Taylor surveying the living room, he cleared his throat.

"Before y'all head out, I've got some things I want you to take back with you," he said.

Taylor noted her father's solemn tone but was distracted trying to keep Parker from pulling off her shoes in the car seat. "Sure Dad, just make it quick, we should already be on the road," she said.

Joe disappeared down the hall and returned with a plain canvas bag. He handed it to Jake, who had come to stand beside Taylor.

"Now I know you think I'm just a paranoid old man," Joe said. "But I'd feel better knowing you have these, just in case."

Curious, Jake unzipped the bag while Joe continued. "It ain't much. Some basic survival supplies. Flashlight, first aid kit. And a handgun with ammo, for protection."

Jake pawed through the bag's contents while Taylor crossed her arms. "Dad..." she said in a weary voice.

"Just hear me out," Joe said, holding up a hand. "The world's getting dangerous. If chaos comes, folks are gonna get desperate. Better you can defend yourselves."

He pointed to a worn map of Florida covered in highlighting and notes. "There's the route to our cabin marked, away from major highways. Avoid the refugees fleeing the cities."

Taylor sighed, exasperated. "You think society is just going to collapse any day? Don't you think you're overreacting a little?"

Joe's jaw tightened. "Maybe, maybe not. But if I'm right, you'll be glad you have these things. And if I'm wrong, no harm keeping them on hand."

"Fine, we'll take the silly bag," Taylor huffed. She headed out to the SUV without another glance.

Jake lingered, meeting Joe's steely gaze. "I'll keep it close," he said quietly. "Better safe than sorry." Joe clasped Jake's shoulder firmly. "You're a good man. Take care of our girls."

Jake gave Joe a solemn nod before heading out to load up the SUV. Taylor was already belted into the passenger seat, scrolling impatiently through her phone.

Joe and Jojo stood in the driveway, waving as the SUV pulled away. When it disappeared from sight, Joe's smile faded. He surveyed the neighborhood streets, alive on this sunny Saturday morning with kids playing and neighbors tending their yards.

Everything seemed normal, but Joe couldn't

ignore the pit in his stomach. He said a silent prayer that the peace and freedom they enjoyed would not be shattered anytime soon. With grim determination, he turned and followed Jojo back inside the house.

With a heavy feeling in his gut, he turned and walked slowly back inside, letting the screen door bang shut behind him. He hoped his nagging sense of dread was just paranoia as Taylor claimed.

But something in his bones told him chaos was on the horizon. And when it came, his family would need to draw on every ounce of strength and courage to survive. All he could do was try and prepare them as best he could.

The rest was in God's hands now. Sending up a silent prayer for their safety, Joe got back to work cleaning his rifle collection. He focused on the task at hand with diligent care and precision. Ready for whatever the future would hold

CHAPTER THREE
ESCAPE FROM THE CITY

O ver the next week, life continued on uneventfully for the Kelly family in Miami. Joe and Jojo kept a watchful eye on the news, but no new threats emerged.

On a sunny Tuesday morning, Joe sat drinking coffee on the back patio. He wore a black cotton T-shirt with the sleeves rolled up and a battered old John Deere cap that had belonged to his father. The salt and pepper stubble on his jaw glittered in the morning sun.

Joe's trained ear detected aircraft passing high overhead. He craned his neck, squinting against the glare. A small formation of military jets streaked across the sky, heading south.

Joe's pulse quickened. In all his years living near Homestead Air Reserve Base, he had never seen warplanes scramble here unless a hurricane was approaching. He stared hard at the empty sky long after the jets had disappeared from sight.

Just then, Jojo hurried out the patio door. "Dad, you gotta come quick - something's happening!"

Joe followed his son back inside to the living room television. They arrived to see panicked newscasters speaking rapidly against a backdrop of the White House being hastily evacuated. Officials were being rushed into bunkers and aircraft could be heard flying low over the capital.

Joe and Jojo exchanged grave looks. This was exactly the type of crisis they had been preparing for. Jojo wordlessly handed his father an emergency bug-out bag and rifle. Joe accepted them, his jaw set.

The television screens abruptly went black. Seconds later, the house lights flickered out, plunging them into darkness. In the distance, alarms wailed as emergency generators kicked in.

"It's an EMP," Joe said through gritted teeth. "A coordinated attack. Just like we feared." His worst predictions were coming true.

Jojo gripped his father's shoulder, his military training taking over. "Let's get moving then. Grab Gram and essential supplies only. We need to get out of the city before chaos erupts."

Joe nodded, steeling himself for the difficult

journey ahead. He took one last look out the window at his neighborhood, peaceful only minutes ago. Now the panicked cries of neighbors could be heard as the disaster began to unfold.

Jaw clenched, Joe turned away and headed upstairs to get his mother. It was time to go.

Toni was in her bedroom getting dressed when Joe came to the door. At eighty, she moved slower these days but was still fiercely independent.

"No need to knock, I'm decent," she called in her smoky voice. Her short silver hair was neatly styled, and she wore slacks and a floral blouse. "Joe, I think the damn power is out again, can you call the power company?"

"Mom, there's an emergency, we need to leave immediately," Joe said urgently.

"What emergency?" She asked.

"Mom, something has happened, Jojo and I think it's an EMP attack." Joe explained

What the hell is an EM, whatever attack?" Toni asked with concern.

"Gram, we don't have time for this, just trust me" Joe implored.

"Slow down son, what exactly are you talking about?" Toni said, now concerned

Joe tried to quickly explain to her, "An EMP, it

stands for Electromagnetic Pulse, basically it fries everything that has electronics in it. That's why we have no power. We were watching them evacuating the White House live on television when all of this happened. Things will deteriorate quickly with no power for a prolonged period of time, that's why we want to get moving before things get really bad here in the city."

Toni stood staring at her son, "Joe, are you sure about all this?"

"Mom, I'm pretty sure, but one thing I know is it's better to be safe than sorry, and Jojo and I think it best to get the hell out of Dodge as soon as possible."

"Well, if there's anybody, I trust more than you and Jojo, I don't know who it would be."

Toni's lined face creased in a frown. "Good Lord. Well don't just stand there, help me pack a suitcase."

"Mom, forget suitcases, only grab what you can carry. I have a feeling we'll be walking cause I think the cars are gonna be dead.

They hastily packed a bag for Toni and Jojo. Joe double-checked his own bug-out bag containing survival supplies, firearms, ammunition and cash.

On their way downstairs, Toni stopped in the living room. Her eyes roamed over the family photos displayed on the walls and shelves. "I hope we'll see our home again someday," she said wistfully.

"We will, Mom," Joe squeezed her narrow shoulder. "But right now, we gotta go."

Outside, a frightening scene greeted them. Neighbors ran about yelling and trying to start disabled cars. Thick black smoke rose in the distance from crashed airplanes and crippled emergency vehicles. The traffic lights were dead.

Jojo had run outside to check the cars. "Yep, dad they're dead alright, looks like we'll be hoofin' it from here on out. He yelled.

Joe turned to his mother and said "Gram I hope you're up for this, this is gonna be a long trip" Toni replied "it is what it is Joe, we'll get through it one way or another.

Hoisting their bags onto their backs, the trio struck out down the sidewalk at a brisk pace. Joe's jaw was set, his eyes hard. After years of waiting and preparing, the day of reckoning had arrived. Now their survival depended on making it out of the stricken city on foot and reaching the sanctuary of their rural cabin.

The journey would test them to their very limits. But Joe knew his family would draw on every ounce of courage and resourcefulness to survive. As Miami fell into anarchy behind them, he steeled himself for the difficult road ahead.

CHAPTER FOUR
DARK DAYS AHEAD

In St. Augustine, Taylor relaxed on the couch while Jake entertained Parker. The toddler squealed happily as Jake made silly faces. Taylor smiled at their antics.

Suddenly the power cut out, plunging the house into darkness. Taylor sat up, surprised.

"Huh, that's weird, oh it must be the end of the world, dad was right" she joked.

Jake tried turning on his phone, but it was dead. "That can't be right, I know I had 50% battery left," he said with a furrowed brow.

Taylor grabbed her own fully charged phone and tossed it over to let Jake use it, but it wouldn't power on either. They exchanged uneasy looks in the darkness.

"What are the odds we both have dead phones at the same time the power goes out?" Taylor said.

Jake felt a twist of anxiety in his gut. He glanced

out the window where neighbors milled about confused. "Let's check the car radio," he suggested.

Outside, their SUV was silent and dead just like the other cars. Jake tried the ignition, but it didn't even click.

Taylor crossed her arms, eyes wide. "Okay this is really freaking me out now. Do you think...could my dad actually have been right?"

Jake ran a hand through his hair. "I don't know, but this doesn't seem normal. We'd better round up the emergency supplies your dad gave us, just to be safe."

Taylor nodded, mind racing. She took Parker from Jake and hurried back inside, a feeling of dread growing in the pit of her stomach. Whatever was happening, she had a bad feeling their lives were about to change dramatically.

CHAPTER FIVE
A GRIM CHOICE

Miles away in Punta Gorda, Florida, Joe's ex-wife Paulette hurried around her small house, anxiously packing a large backpack. Her hands shook slightly as she stuffed in a few changes of clothes, toiletries, and a framed photo of her grown children Taylor and Jojo. Slinging the heavy bag over her shoulder, she took one last look at the dark, silent trailer before stepping outside.

Ever since the power had abruptly gone out, Paulette had a dreadful feeling in the pit of her stomach that something terrible was unfolding. With her phone dead, she had no way to reach her kids. All she could do was try to make her way north to their father's remote cabin, praying they would eventually show up there too. While she wasn't Joe's favorite person, she believed he was a good man with a good heart and would surely take her in if she could just make it to the cabin.

Paulette was used to being on her feet all day from working waitress jobs over the years, but what lay ahead, a walk from Punta Gorda to Lake Harris, this was going to be grueling. She took a deep breath to gather her courage. At 58, she was still spry and strong-willed thanks to years of surviving a hard life. She was leaving nothing behind really. A rickety, leaking old trailer she called home for the past several years, and with no possessions to speak of. Drawing on all her resolve now, she started walking steadily northeast, following backroads away from the center of town. Her destination was 200 miles away over rough rural terrain. With transportation disabled, she was facing an arduous journey on foot. But Paulette was not one to back down from a challenge. She would do whatever it took to be reunited with her family.

The road stretched on for miles, empty except for a few bewildered strangers wandering aimlessly. Paulette kept her distance, avoiding eye contact. The isolation suited her; it allowed her to focus inward. She had always been independent and self-sufficient. Now she would rely on those traits more than ever to see her through this crisis alone.

As twilight descended, Paulette found an abandoned shed to spend the night. Too exhausted to eat, she lay awake staring into the darkness, thoughts racing. Had Joe and Jojo made it out of Miami? Were they safe? Would Taylor go to the cabin or remain her stubborn self and try to stick it out in St. Augustine? She had to believe her stubborn ex-husband would lead their family through this. Eventually, they would all find their way to the cabin. Until then, she could only keep putting one foot in front of the other.

Her journey had just begun, but already Paulette could feel her courage and resilience rising to meet this new world. Whatever lay ahead, she would face it with her characteristic grit and indomitable spirit. Somehow, against all odds, she would be reunited with her children.

CHAPTER SIX
INTO THE WILDERNESS

As night fell over the rural Krome Avenue, Joe squinted into the growing darkness.

"We need to find a spot to camp soon," he said gruffly. "Before it gets too dark to see."

Jojo peered down the empty road, then into the thick woods lining it. "Doesn't seem to be any clearings nearby. We might have to just pull off at the roadside."

Toni shook her head anxiously. "I don't like the idea of sleeping right on the edge of the swamp. Too many critters wandering around at night that can get at us."

Joe sighed. "You're right, Ma. But I don't think we have much choice. This terrain is too overgrown."

Reluctantly, Joe led them off the road under some trees. As Jojo gathered kindling for a fire, Toni frowned at the damp, muddy ground.

"Oh goodness, we'll catch our death sleeping on

this wet soil!"

"I'll find some leaves and pine needles to lay down as bedding," Joe assured her. "It's better than nothing."

Soon Jojo had a small fire crackling. As Toni and Jojo ate from their dwindling provisions, Joe spread out the makeshift bedding he had gathered.

"C'mon now, it's getting late. Let's turn in," he said gruffly.

Toni lay down gingerly on the lumpy leaf pile. "Oh, my aching back won't like this one bit."

"Just try to rest, Gram," Jojo said gently. "We'll be somewhere more comfortable soon."

As the night deepened, strange sounds echoed from the swamp. Toni shivered. "Good lord, what was that? An alligator?"

"Could be anything," Joe said. "But the fire will keep them back. Get some sleep."

After a few fretful hours, Joe shook Jojo awake for the next watch. "Here, take the rifle. Anything moves out there, you shoot first, and ask questions later."

"You got it, Dad," Jojo said, taking his position.

At dawn, Jojo roused the others. "Rise and shine. We should get moving."

Joe groaned as he sat up stiffly. "Feels like I just

closed my eyes. But you're right, we need to cover some ground today."

As they walked, Toni reminisced fondly about Jojo and Joe's childhood adventures. Jojo laughed. "Remember that time I fell in the canal chasing a frog? Boy, were you mad, Dad."

"Had to walk you home sopping wet! Your mother thought it was a hoot though." Joe said, smiling.

At a roadside car, Joe said "Let's check it quickly for supplies." Inside, he found only an old atlas. "Here Jojo, maybe you can use this to navigate us on backroads."

"Good idea, Pops. I'll study it tonight." Jojo said, tucking it into his bag.

At their next stop, Toni smiled wearily. "My feet are barking something fierce. But I'm still kicking, don't you worry about me."

Joe patted her shoulder. "You're tougher than you look, Ma. We'll get you to the cabin just fine."

Toni chuckled. "I may be slow, but I've still got some life in these old bones."

Joe nodded. "That you do. Now let's get moving again."

CHAPTER SEVEN
SHELTER IN PLACE

It had been a long, exhausting day of chaos and uncertainty ever since the power went out. The entire region was still without electricity, cell service was non-existent, and rumors were flying about some kind of attack or catastrophic event. They had walked to stock up on basics at the store, only to find anxious crowds and bare shelves, the tension in the air palpable.

Taylor sank into the sofa, rubbing her temples as she tried to make sense of it all. She had written off her father as an eccentric doomsday prepper, stockpiling for imaginary disasters in his secure cabin. Now his dire warnings seemed less far-fetched. But what exactly did he know that they didn't?

Jake stood with his hands on his hips, brows knitted as he took in their haul. "I guess your dad was right about stocking up while we still could," he said. "Don't know how much longer the stores will stay open if this keeps up."

Taylor sighed, the panicked mob at the supermarket still fresh in her mind. "At least we got enough to last us a little while if things get really crazy." She paused, chewing her bottom lip. "Do you think he was also right about...you know, getting out of the city?"

Jake met her gaze, seeing his own fear reflected there. "Honestly? I don't know. But I don't like how everything's looking right now."

They sat in tense silence for several minutes, the weight of Joe's warning hanging over them. Taylor's mind spun with terrifying hypotheticals as she glanced around at the comfortable suburban home, they'd worked so hard for. The idea of leaving it all behind and heading off into the unknown made her palms sweat.

Finally, she spoke up again, her voice quiet. "Jake...I hate to say it, but I'm starting to think the old man might have been right after all."

Jake nodded slowly, thinking it over. "I'm glad you said it first, because I was thinking the same thing. Your dad's a character, but he's not an idiot. If he says we need to get out of Dodge, maybe we should listen."

Taylor buried her face in her hands with a groan. This went against every fiber of her being. She and Joe had clashed for years over his zealous preparedness for doomsday scenarios she found absurd. The idea of actually taking his advice and bugging out to his remote cabin compound was enough to make her scream.

Jake sat down and wrapped an arm around her, kissing the top of her head. "I know this is scary, babe. Believe me, I do. But we need to consider it. Your dad clearly knows stuff we don't. And there is one thing I know for sure, your dad cares about family more than anything."

Taylor took a deep breath, slowly looking up. "You really think we should do this? Head to Dad's cabin like he said?"

"I don't know if we have any other choice. He seems to have predicted all this so far. We need to trust him on the next steps." Jake furrowed his brow, thinking hard. "In fact, didn't he give you one of those bug-out bags a while back? Just in case?"

Taylor's eyes widened. She jumped up and ran down the hall to grab the military-grade backpack stashed in their bedroom closet. Hauling it onto the table, she and Jake sat examining the contents: maps, protein bars, water purification tablets, flashlights, a first aid kit, pocketknives, and survival guides.

Despite herself, Taylor felt a surge of gratitude for her dad's tireless preparedness. This bag alone would give them a fighting chance, filled with supplies that could now mean the difference between life or death if society continued to unravel at this pace.

She traced her fingers over the topo maps, hiking trails highlighted in pink marker. "Look at this. He mapped out detailed evacuation routes to his cabin. That sneaky old goat." She shook her head with a sad smile.

Jake let out an incredulous chuckle. "Well, I'll be damned. Your dad really does have his ducks in a row." He turned to Taylor with a somber expression. "I think this settles it, hon. We need to go."

Taylor chewed her lip, emotions swirling - fear, anger, sadness. This wasn't how things were supposed to be. But Jake was right - they were out of options. She took a deep breath and squeezed his hand, meeting his resolute gaze.

"Okay. We'll do it. At first light tomorrow, we'll follow one of these routes' dad mapped out. Hopefully we can make it to the cabin safely." Her voice broke as she glanced around their home once more, wishing with all her heart this was just a bad dream. But she quickly steeled herself. Their survival was all that mattered now.

Jake pulled her to him gently. "We're going to get through this, Taylor. Together. I love you." He kissed the top of her head again as she clung to him, taking comfort in his solid strength.

They stayed like that for a long moment before pulling apart and getting to work. Quiet intensity filled the air as they sorted supplies, packed essentials, and planned their route using Joe's maps. They moved with urgency, but their motions were heavy - each task a bitter farewell to the world they knew.

Finally, they collapsed into bed, the gravity of what they would set out to do at sunrise weighing on them. Jake wrapped Taylor tightly in his arms, and she nestled into his chest, finding solace in his heartbeat as her own heart grieved for all they were leaving behind. Somehow, some way, they would make it through this. They had to.

CHAPTER EIGHT
GRABBIN' GRAM SOME WHEELS

The early morning sun peeked over the horizon, casting its warm glow and rousing Joe from a restless slumber. He groaned as he sat up, joints creaking and back aching after another night spent on the hard ground. Running a hand through his salt and pepper hair, he looked over at his son Jojo and mother Toni, both still fast asleep. He hated to wake them, but they had to get moving.

"Rise and shine," Joe said, gently shaking Jojo's shoulder.

Jojo snorted awake, eyes darting around for a moment before he got his bearings. At 33, he was in his physical prime, but the nonstop stress of their journey north had taken its toll mentally. Still, he always quickly rebounded thanks to his military training.

"Are we close to Clewiston?" Jojo asked, voice gravelly with sleep.

Joe nodded. "Should be there sometime tomorrow, if we make good time."

They'd been traveling on foot for days now, ever since the EMP wiped out anything electronic. No more modern conveniences like cars or cell phones. Just their two feet and whatever supplies they could scavenge along the way. It was a grueling trek made worse by his mother's age. But they had to keep going, had to get Toni to the safety of his cabin up north.Speaking of his mother, Joe shuffled over to gently shake her shoulder too. "Rise and shine, Ma. We gotta get moving."

Toni's eyes fluttered open, glazed and confused for a moment before awareness set in. "Joseph," she muttered, "just five more minutes."

He chuckled despite himself. Even at 80 years old, she was still stubborn as a mule. "Come on now, we've slept enough. Let's get you up."

With Jojo's help, they carefully got Toni to her feet. She stood hunched and frail, but with a determined glint in her eyes. His strong-willed mother hadn't let her bum hip or anything else slow her down yet. Joe prayed she could keep the pace again today.

After a quick breakfast of canned beans, they packed up their gear and set off down the empty highway. The sun continued its ascent, washing the abandoned cars and trucks in a golden glow. It would've been beautiful if not for the eerie silence that hung over the land. Not so much as a bird chirping anywhere.

Joe did his best to fill the void with lighthearted banter, telling stories of his youth that he knew would get a rise out of Toni. She never missed a chance to give him a little verbal jab, often to Jojo's amusement. The playful family dynamic helped distract them from the dire reality of their circumstances.

They had been walking for a couple hours when Toni started severely lagging behind. Joe could see her limp becoming more pronounced, the pain etched across her weathered face with each labored step.

"How about a quick break?" he suggested, trying to mask his worry.

"No, no, I'm fine," Toni insisted, even as she swayed unsteadily. "Let's keep going."

Joe opened his mouth to protest when Jojo suddenly stopped short up ahead. "Hold up. I think I see something."

He shuffled over to a battered sedan and peered inside. After a moment, he smashed the rear window with his elbow, reaching in to wrestle something out.

Joe hurried over, concerned and confused. "What the hell are you doing?"

When Jojo turned around, he was holding a collapsed wheelchair. "I had an idea."

It took Joe a moment to register what he was seeing. Then a grin spread across his face. "My boy, you're a goddamn genius!"

Jojo quickly unfolded the wheelchair while Joe helped Toni hobble over. "Gram, your chariot awaits." As soon as she sank into the seat, an immense look of relief washed over her features.

"Oh, this is heavenly," she sighed. "Bless you, Jojo."

Pride swelled in Joe's chest as he squeezed his son's shoulder. "That's my boy. Always looking out for his gram."

Jojo rubbed the back of his neck, a hint of a smile teasing his lips. "Well, we still have a long way to go. Might as well make the trip a little easier on her."

"A little easier is an understatement!" Toni quipped. "Now I can relax and enjoy the sights while you boys do all the work pushing me along."

They all shared a much-needed laugh at that. With Toni comfortably situated in the wheelchair, they continued their trek up the empty highway. The miles seemed to pass much easier now, especially when Toni dozed off for a stretch. Joe kept a vigilant watch for threats, but thankfully encountered none.

By late afternoon, storm clouds were gathering overhead. Joe eyed them warily as a stiff breeze kicked up.

"Let's start looking for a place to hunker down for the night," he said.

CHAPTER NINE
LEAVING ST. AUGUSTINE

The early morning sun crept through the bedroom windows, bathing the room in a harsh golden light. Taylor blinked awake, at once feeling the oppressive heat settling over them. Without air conditioning, the house was sweltering already.

Beside her Jake stirred, kicking the thin sheet off his legs with a grunt. "So much for sleeping in," he muttered.

Taylor sat up, raking a hand through her messy brown locks. "No kidding. It's like an oven in here."

Jake swung his legs off the bed and walked over to the window, peering out at the street down below. "Doesn't look like anyone has power. The whole block is dark."

"No surprise there," Taylor sighed. She checked her wristwatch out of habit before remembering it had stopped days ago. "What time do you think it is?"

Jake shrugged. "Sun's just up so maybe 6 or 7 am? Hard to tell without clocks." He turned back to Taylor. "We should get ready to leave soon, before it gets any hotter."

After a quick breakfast of lukewarm canned fruit eaten in the stuffy kitchen, Taylor and Jake began the process of packing their supplies one by one. They went over Joe's list over and over, debating each item in hushed voices before carefully stowing it into their hiking packs.

"Bring the first aid kit or the fishing gear?" Jake asked, holding up both.

"First aid kit for sure," Taylor decided. "We can try fishing when we get there."

It was a tedious but necessary process. Flashlights, batteries, clothing, canned goods, bottled water, blankets. The packs grew heavier by the minute.

Jake lifted his bag with a huff. "We're going to be hauling a ton of gear through this heat."

"Dad would say it's better to have too much than too little," Taylor said as she re-checked the supplies. Her father was right - better safe than sorry out in the wilderness. "Also, he gave us that gun and boxes of ammunition, I'll let you carry that I- I just don't know that I could be able to shoot someone. Taylor remarked. Jake said, frankly sweetie, I don't know if I could bring myself to do it either, but if it meant protecting you and Parker, I'll find the strength somehow.

Joe had left them more than just a supply list. At the very bottom of the duffel bag was a detailed map, marked with two potential routes to the cabin's remote location. Jake spread it open on the kitchen counter, pondering it with a furrowed brow.

"Looks like your dad recommends we avoid Palatka and take the southern route, through Bunnell," Jake said. "Says it will be safer."

Taylor traced the winding back roads with her finger. She had no doubt her father's advice was sound. If Joe said Bunnell was the way to go, then that's what they would do. The route veered south, the journey lengthening their trip by half a day, but reaching the cabin intact was all that mattered.

"Then Bunnell it is," Taylor said with a sharp nod.

The last task was packing for the most important cargo - her two-year-old daughter, Parker. They filled her little pink backpack with extra diapers, wipes, a few favorite toys and books. Parker watched them with curiosity, blissfully unaware of what was happening. Looking at her cherubic face made Taylor's throat tighten with emotion. They had to keep her safe, no matter what.

Finally, as the sun crawled higher in the sky, they shouldered their packs and headed for the door. With glistening eyes, they turned and took one last look inside their home. They were abandoning everything they had worked so hard for, but safety was the highest priority now and with that thought, they walked out the front door. Jake locked it behind them out of habit, though Taylor doubted anyone was going to break in. The neighborhood seemed like a ghost town; front doors left gaping open on several of the other homes on their street. Jake noticed a few neighbors peeping from windows at them as they began their perilous journey.

Jake took Parker's hand as they walked down the deserted street. "Here we go, little one. Big adventure ahead."

The curly haired toddler skipped along, smiling. "Advencher! Yay!" she cheered.

Taylor's lips quirked. If only she could share in her daughter's carefree excitement. Right now, the journey felt like anything but a cheerful adventure. But she had to keep faith that her father's instructions would lead them through.

Step by cautious step, they made their way out of the suburbs and onto a rural highway. Here the trees and overgrown brush encroached on either side, the world around them seeming somehow wilder. Taylor took a deep breath, adjusting the pack on her shoulders. It was time to trust in her father and keep her family safe, no matter what perils lay ahead. They were on their way.

CHAPTER TEN
A CHANCE ENCOUNTER

After a miserable night hunkering down in an abandoned car for the night to get out of the rainstorm everyone was stiff and cranky.

Joe and Jojo took turns pushing Toni in her wheelchair down the cracked asphalt road. The midday Florida sun beat down relentlessly, making their progress slow and laborious.

"Ow, this blasted chair is so bumpy and uncomfortable," Toni complained as they hit another pothole. "Couldn't you boys have found me something better to ride in?"

"Sorry Ma, this was the only one we could get on short notice," Joe replied, wiping sweat from his brow. "Just try and bear with it - this is the fastest way we can travel right now."

Joe was thankful they had managed to secure

the wheelchair for Toni along the way. There was no way the elderly woman could have managed the long trek on foot. But that didn't make her any less cantankerous about their mode of transportation.

They continued on, the baked asphalt shimmering in the heat. They were traveling on back roads and had only encountered a few groups of people along the way. The people were all headed in the opposite direction, back toward the city. Joe figured after their cars died these people, unaware of what was happening, started walking back to their homes. He felt bad for them, the city was not going to be a good place to be in the very near future. Things would get bad there as soon as everyone finally figured it out, no help was coming.

As they reached the outskirts of South Bay Jojo held up a hand.

"I see a car up ahead, about half a mile up," he said, squinting. "Looks like there's someone next to it."

Joe took the binoculars from Jojo's backpack and peered ahead. Near a stranded sedan, a lone figure paced back and forth. He could make out a woman's form, but no one else.

"Just one person that I can see, maybe female," Joe said. "But keep your eyes open, could be an ambush

They moved forward warily, scoping the surroundings for any sign of danger. As they drew closer, it became clear the woman was alone on the deserted road. Still, they approached with caution, hands ready by their weapons just in case.

"Are you okay?" Joe called out when they were twenty yards away.

The woman turned, relief flooding her face. "Oh, thank God," she cried. "My car died a couple of days ago and I didn't know what to do. Please, can you help me?"

She looked to be in her late thirties or early forties, Joe observed. His eyes swept over her curvy figure appreciatively before he checked himself.

"Yeah, seems to be a lot of that going around lately," he said as they reached her.

"I don't understand what's happening," the woman said, her voice trembling. "I was driving home to Leesburg when everything just cut out. My phone, my car, everything's dead. I've been waiting here hoping someone could help but no one's passed by until you."

"We're thinking it was some kind of EMP strike, knocking out the power grid and electronics," Joe explained. "Whatever it was, help ain't coming.

We're on our own out here."

He nodded towards Toni and Jojo. "I'm Joe, this is my mother Toni and my son Jojo. We're heading north ourselves to the same area you're heading to actually, hoping to meet up with more of our family."

"Oh gosh, I'm so sorry, I haven't even introduced myself," the woman said. "I'm Maria."

Joe chuckled. "Well, what do you know, my ma's middle name just happens to be Maria too. Must be your lucky day running into us."

Toni shot him a look that said not to get too friendly. But Joe was already envisioning the alluring Maria joining their group. An extra gun hand wouldn't hurt, plus she seemed capable enough to pull her weight. And easy on the eyes too...

Maria flashed a grateful smile, looking over them hopefully. "Is there any way I could travel with you? I don't know how I'd ever make it back to Leesburg on my own."

Toni pursed her lips skeptically, but Jojo nodded. "Of course, we'd be glad to have you join us. Right Dad?""Sure, the more the merrier," Joe said, returning Maria's smile. "We're just happy to help someone in need."

"Thank you all so much," Maria gushed. "I don't know what I would have done stranded out here alone. I've had to sleep in my car, thank God I had a couple of fast-food burgers I had picked up for the road trip, but I am parched, do you possibly have a little water you could spare, I swear I'll find a way to repay your kindness, I promise."

"Don't even mention it," Joe said as he grabbed a water bottle and handed it to her with a smile. "Let's take a look at what supplies you've got, and we'll see about getting back on the road. Safety in numbers after all."

Maria popped the trunk of her car and began showing them her gear. Joe watched her intently as she and Jojo took stock. He felt his pulse quicken looking at her. Having an attractive new woman along for the ride might make their endless trek a bit more enjoyable, he mused.

Of course, he'd have to keep his desires in check and remain focused on the task at hand - getting his family to safety. But a man has needs, and Joe could certainly think of a few ways lovely Maria could repay her debt. He shook the thought from his mind. Time enough for that later.

"Alright, looks like you've got some useful things here," Jojo said, snapping Joe's attention back to the present. "Let's divvy it up and hit the road."

Joe took over pushing Toni's wheelchair while Jojo and Maria distributed her supplies into their packs. Within ten minutes, they were back moving down the highway, their party now increased to four. Joe made sure to take the lead, able to glance back periodically and admire their shapely new companion.

Yes, having Maria along would certainly make the hot, grueling days ahead more bearable, he thought. Their journey was far from over, but Joe's spirits were already lifted.

CHAPTER ELEVEN
A STRANGERS WARNING

The morning sun filtered through the trees as Jake, Taylor and little Parker made their way south along the edge of highway US 1. They had set out at first light, eager to get moving on the thirty-mile trek to Bunnell where they would pick up highway 11 and continue further south.

The highway was jammed with broken down cars and crowds of people wandering listlessly along the pavement. Many were begging passing travelers for food or water. Just days before, these people were their neighbors, fellow townspeople, now they seemed more like zombies wandering around aimlessly. The cries of the desperate and destitute echoed through the air, a sorrowful soundtrack to this strange new world.

Jake led the way, cutting through the dense forest parallel to the road. He wanted to avoid contact with the masses as much as possible. The scene was simply too chaotic and unpredictable.

Little Parker clung to her momma's back; her skinny legs wrapped tightly around Taylor's waist. At two years old, she was blissfully unaware of the peril around them.

Taylor stroked her daughter's fine blonde hair and planted a kiss on her cheek as they walked. "You be a good girl now, "P". We've got a long way to go."

They trudged on for a couple of more miles without incident. The heavy forest brush made the going slow. Jake took the lead while Taylor followed close behind, one hand pressed against Parker's back to keep her steady.

By midday, the Florida heat was sweltering. They took a short break under the shade of a sprawling live oak. Jake pulled out a bottle of water and took a small sip before passing it to Taylor.

"Go easy," he said. "Only got a few bottles left."

Taylor nodded and took a careful swig before lifting Parker for a tiny sip. After their short rest, they pressed on through the woods.

Around a half mile later, they stumbled upon a man sprawled on the forest floor just off the highway. One leg was crudely bandaged with a bloody rag tied around his thigh.

"Please..." he croaked. "Help me."

Jake hesitated, exchanging a wary glance with Taylor.

"Jake, we have to do something," Taylor said.

Jake let out a short sigh. He knelt down and examined the man's leg. The wound didn't look too severe, but it needed proper dressing. Taylor offered her overshirt and Jake used it to tightly bind the man's thigh.

"Here, take some water," Taylor said, handing the man her bottle.

"Thank you, bless you both," he said weakly as he gulped down the water. "There are bad men up ahead, patrolling the highway...gangs. You'd do well to avoid it."

Jake's jaw tightened. He hadn't counted on dealing with gangs.

"Let's get moving," Jake said tersely, helping the man sit up against a tree. It was a struggle to show kindness in this lawless new world. But it helped ensure his own humanity remained intact.

Taking the injured man's warning to heart, Jake led his family deeper into the thick forest, miles away from the exposed highway where gangs now waited. It was tortuous terrain, full of thorns and tangled vines that threatened to ensnare their ankles. But they pushed forward steadily, surviving not just the elements but their own deepest fears. Jake focused on his purpose, step by step - keeping his loved ones safe.

CHAPTER TWELVE
SENSING DANGER

Taylor and Jake walked slowly down the deserted highway, cautiously scanning the wooded areas on either side for any signs of danger. It had been days since the EMP blast wiped out power across the country, leaving them stranded far from home and family.

Taylor broke the silence. "I can't believe this is really happening. I always thought dad was paranoid when he talked about being prepared for disaster. I never took it seriously."

Jake nodded somberly. "Yeah, I know. I figured Joe was a little extreme too. Now I'm kicking myself for not listening more. If anything happens to you or Parker..." His voice trailed off, choked with emotion.

He stopped walking and turned to face Taylor, taking her hands in his. "I swear to you, I'm going to step up and take care of my family. We'll get through this. Once we reach your dad's cabin. I'll learn everything I can from Joe and Jojo about survival, and how to protect you both."

Taylor's eyes glistened with tears. She leaned forward, resting her head on Jake's chest. "I'm so scared for us," she whispered. "This world now... it's like my worst nightmares come true."

Jake held her close, stroking her long hair. "We'll make it, babe. We'll pull together and get through this. I promise you."

After a long moment, Taylor lifted her head and gazed up at Jake. "I feel so guilty that I didn't spend more time with Dad and Jojo before all this. They tried to warn me to be prepared. Maybe if I'd listened more, I could help us now."

"You can't blame yourself," Jake said firmly. "None of us saw this coming. But we're together, and that's what matters. Your family is going to need you...we all will. You're one of the strongest people I know."

Taylor managed a small, sad smile. "When did you get so wise, huh?"

Jake chuckled softly. "I've always been wise; you just didn't appreciate my wisdom!"

The brief moment of levity lifted their spirits. Taylor took Jake's hand again and they continued walking, freshly resolved to endure whatever lay ahead.

As they approached the outskirts of the next small town, they slowed their pace, carefully surveying the abandoned buildings. Nothing moved except a stray dog scrounging for scraps. The eerie silence raised the hairs on the back of Taylor's neck.

Jake put a protective arm around her. "Let's check some of these stores for supplies quickly and get back on the road. I don't like the feel of this place."

They slipped into the first store they came to, a small mom-and-pop market. Inside, shelves were ransacked and spilled contents covered the floor.

Jake shook his head. "Looks like this place was already raided. But let's take a look around just in case."

Working their way down each aisle, they scoured for anything usable - food, batteries, tools. In one corner, they discovered several unpacked cases of canned soup. "Jackpot!" Jake exclaimed. "This will keep us fed for a while."

As they exited the market, loaded down with supplies, the ominous feeling returned. Taylor's muscles tensed and she held Parker tighter to her chest. "Jake, I think we're being watched. Let's hurry."

They moved quickly back to the main road. Taylor's heart pounded as she felt invisible eyes tracking them. She glanced back and saw two men emerging from an alley, staring after them.

"Faster, Jake!" Taylor said urgently. They broke into a jog, not stopping until the town was out of sight.

CHAPTER THIRTEEN
A CLOSE CALL

Joe and Jojo continued walking down the deserted highway, their bags slung over their shoulders, eyes scanning the landscape for any signs of danger. The late morning sun beat down on them as they trudged along the cracked asphalt.

Joe glanced over at his son, a wry smile crossing his bearded face. "So, what do you think of our new companion?" he asked, jerking his thumb back at Maria.

Jojo chuckled, adjusting the rifle strap on his shoulder. "Oh, I think she'll be a valuable addition to our merry little band."

"Is that right?" Joe raised an eyebrow.

"Yeah. I mean she's smart, seems capable. And it doesn't hurt that she's smokin' hot," Jojo added with a sly grin.

Joe scoffed. "It ain't like that between us. I just appreciate the extra company is all."

"Uh huh. Sure, Dad. You could use a little "company," Jojo said, using air quotes. "I think it's probably been a long time since you've had a little company."

"Alright, that's enough out of you, ya little shit," Joe snapped, though there was no real anger behind it. "You're a real smartass, you know that?"

Jojo chuckled again. "Yes sir, it's a specialty of mine."

Their playful banter trailed off as a new sound reached their ears - a low, rumbling roar, steadily growing louder. Joe tensed, his hand automatically going to the revolver on his hip.

"You hear that?" he murmured.

Jojo nodded, his smile vanishing. He turned to scan the road behind them.

In the distance, three motorcycles crested a hill, speeding along the highway. As they drew nearer, the sounds of sporadic gunfire echoed through the air.

"Ah hell," Joe growled. "Take cover, now!"

He waved the others off the road toward some scraggly bushes and eroded gullies, hoping to get out of sight. But it was too late. The bikers had spotted them, angling in their direction as they raced closer.

With a squeal of brakes, the motorcycles skidded to a stop, circling around the group in a cloud of dust and exhaust. Hard-looking men wielding an array of firearms glared at them menacingly.

Joe's jaw clenched as he subtly shifted to shield the others.

"Well, well...what do we have here?" said the rider closest to Joe - a muscular, bald man with a salt-and-pepper beard and a jagged scar across his left cheekbone. His cold eyes sized them up.

"Just passing through," Joe said gruffly. "We don't want any trouble."

"Sure, sure," Scarface replied, smirking. He jerked his shotgun toward their bags. "Got anything useful in there? Food? Ammo? Medicine?"

"Not much, just some personal items. We ain't got much to spare."

"Now why don't I quite believe you..." Scarface said softly, menace edging his tone. "I think you're holding out on us. So, let's try this again - give us everything you've got, nice and slow, and maybe we'll let you walk away from this."

The other riders tensed as well, aiming their guns steadily. Jojo's jaw clenched, his muscles coiling. He could try to go for his rifle, but they were clearly outnumbered and outgunned.

"There's no need for this," Joe tried again, hands raised. "We can talk-"

"I'm done talking!" Scarface barked, as he dismounted his bike and walked straight towards Maria. He reached her and ran his hand across her face and stroked her hair while smiling. "Now hand over the goddamn supplies before I splatter your brains across the-"

His words cut off with a gurgle as Maria suddenly pulled a knife out of what seemed to be nowhere and lunged at him, plunging the knife into his throat. Scarlet blood sprayed as he fell to his knees.

Chaos erupted.

The bikers opened fire as Jojo and Joe scrambled for their weapons. Maria grabbed Toni's wheelchair, pushing her to cover.

Jojo tackled the nearest biker, struggling to wrestle his shotgun away. The man was younger and stronger though, growling as he pinned Jojo down, about to smash his face with the stock.

But suddenly the biker jerked back with a scream - Joe had put a bullet in the back of his head and blood sprayed all over Jojo as he laid under the biker.

The last biker rushed frantically back to his ride

while Joe took aim and fired. A sudden blast of heat hit them all as Joe's bullet hit the motorcycle's gas tank and exploded killing the last rider instantly.

As the dust settled, Jojo hurried to help Toni, who lay dazed on the ground. Blood seeped from a cut on her forehead, but she gave him a faint smile. Maria quickly moved to treat the wound.

Toni reached up and grasped Jojo's hand with surprising strength. "Thank you," she said hoarsely. "You saved my life; you all saved my life. Thank you, thank you, thank you."

Jojo squeezed her hand gently. "Anytime, Gram."

As a tense silence continued, the group was on alert for any further threats. As the adrenaline rush faded, Joe blew out a long breath, rolling his shoulders to relieve the tension.

"Maria, You Da Man!" Jojo shouted gleefully. "Where did that come from, I thought you were just a good-looking meek librarian type?"

Maria chuckled at Jojo's comment "Meek? uh, not me, hardly. Librarian? Not even close, but at the risk of my own vanity, I'll take the good-looking part. Whether it's true or not, I'll leave for others to decide."

Joe watched the exchange and silently muttered

under his breath, "Oh it's true, oh boy is it true."

Jojo, hearing his dad muttering, shouted, "What's that dad, say something?"

"Nothing son, nothing." Joe replied, grinning. He then turned more serious.

"We gotta be more careful from here on out," he rumbled, glancing back at the others protectively. "No telling what other kind of vermin we'll run into."

Jojo nodded. After seeing how ruthless some had become after the EMP, he knew their journey would only get more treacherous from here. But they would face it together - and heaven help anyone who tried to harm his family.

CHAPTER FOURTEEN
JAKE'S RAGE

The early morning sun filtered through the trees, casting a dappled light on Jake, Taylor and little Parker as they continued their journey on foot through the dense forest. Jake could tell by the growls coming from his and Taylor's stomachs that they needed to find some breakfast soon. Their supplies were running low.

"We've got to start looking for water," Jake said. "The bottles are nearly empty. We should use those purification tablets Joe gave us."

Taylor nodded, shifting Parker from one hip to the other. The two-year-old was getting heavy but Taylor didn't complain. She scanned the woods as they walked, searching for any sign of a stream or pond.

Suddenly a gunshot rang out in the distance, startling birds from their roosts. Jake and Taylor exchanged glances. Jake put his finger to his lips and motioned for Taylor to follow him quietly.

They moved stealthily through the brush toward the sound.

Crouching behind a large oak, they peered ahead at a clearing. Two rugged men with guns stood over a young woman kneeling on the ground. The woman's hands were bound, and her face streaked with tears.

"Please, I don't have anything!" she sobbed as the men yelled and taunted her.

Rage boiled up inside Jake. He clenched his fists, ready to rush in, but Taylor grabbed his arm, her eyes pleading. Protecting Parker had to come first.

Jake gritted his teeth, his protective instincts ignited. "I'm going in," he told Taylor. "I can't let this happen."

One of the men suddenly ripped open the woman's shirt, exposing her bra, then saying, "Oh don't sell yourself short sweetheart, looks like you've got plenty of what I want."

That was the last straw for Jake. He couldn't stand by any longer. Kissing Taylor and Parker quickly, he disappeared into the brush before Taylor could object any further. She hunkered down, holding her daughter close.

Jake crept through the trees until he had a clear

shot. Taking a deep breath, he aimed his trembling hands and pulled the trigger. The shot went wide.

The men whirled, pointing their guns toward the trees. Jake fired again and this time hit one of the men in the leg.

The man let out an agonized scream and collapsed. His partner blindly shot back in Jake's direction. The bullet narrowly missed Jake's head.

Taking careful aim, Jake squeezed off another round but missed. The unwounded assailant tried to take cover while wildly returning fire. Jake's next two shots also went wide.

Finally on his fifth shot, Jake's aim proved true. The second man clutched his chest and crumpled to the ground.

"Stay there!" Jake called out to Taylor. With his gun raised, he cautiously approached the sobbing young woman. The man Jake had wounded was begging pitifully for his life. Jake quietly fired a round into his skull to finish him off.

The woman looked up with large, stunned eyes as Jake neared. He gently helped her to her feet and spoke soothingly, checking her for injuries. After a moment, Taylor slowly appeared from the trees with Parker.

"Thank you," the woman choked out through

sobs. "They ambushed me on the road. They were going to...to..." She couldn't bring herself to say the words.

Jake's heart ached for her. "It's okay, you're safe now," he said softly.

"I'm Jake, this is my wife Taylor and our daughter Parker." He paused. "We're headed to my father-in-law's place. Are you alone?"

"Yes, I'm alone. My name's Claire." the young woman said in a trembling voice. "I was trying to find my brother Miguel; his house is over there. When I got to his place these two scumbags were squatting in his house. I ran to get away, but they caught me, and then you showed up. I'm just worried about where my brother might be."

Jake looked at Taylor and back at Claire. "You can come with us if you've got nowhere to go. I don't think it's really safe for you to stay here all alone"

Taylor gave a reluctant nod. She was still wary of the stranger but couldn't leave the poor girl alone in the state she was in.

"I... I don't have anyone or anywhere to go. Thank you for saving me." She broke down in tears again. "But I should leave a note for my brother as to where I have gone, just in case he should make his way back home, would that be, okay?"

"Yeah, I think that would be fine." Jake said, "Hopefully he will be able to catch up with you at some point."

They scoured the dead men's belongings and recovered some supplies and ammo. Claire mentioned she knew of a creek up ahead they could use to replenish their water. She seemed eager to help, wanting to repay their kindness.

They found the creek and refilled their bottles, adding purification tablets to be safe. Claire proved to know useful survival skills like removing fish from the water with her bare hands. She caught several trout for them to cook up.

By unspoken agreement, they decided to make camp in the woods for the night. Claire started a fire while Taylor prepared the fish in foil packets. Nobody felt much like talking. It had been an emotionally draining day.

As Jake gazed into the crackling fire, he felt good about his decision to rescue Claire but uncertain what the future held.

Sitting close beside Parker, Taylor's mind was also restless. She was relieved they had survived another day, but Claire's presence added new tensions. She knew nothing about their new tagalong, only that she was clearly younger than they were. She figured Claire to be around twenty-two or maybe twenty-five or so. One thing was for sure, Claire was certainly a beautiful girl which raised a tinge of jealousy. Taylor resolved to stay vigilant - her focus had to remain on protecting her little girl, no matter what.

Come morning, the trio would leave a note for Claire's brother and then continue their journey with their new companion. But as Taylor lay listening to the strange night sounds of the forest, she wondered uneasily whether Claire could really be trusted. Exhaustion finally claimed her, along with a deep sleep.

CHAPTER FIFTEEN
GOOD FORTUNE

After the tense confrontation on the road, Joe took a deep breath and turned to the others.

"Okay guys, as much as what just happened really sucks, we now have a couple of options here," he said, gesturing to the two motorcycles lying idle near the bodies of their previous owners.

Jojo wiped blood spatter off his hands onto his pants. "What do you mean, dad?"

"I mean we've now got two functioning motorcycles that these guys aren't going to be needing anymore," Joe explained. He walked over to one of the bikes, an older Harley model, and wheeled it upright. After a quick inspection, he confirmed the key was still in the ignition.

"I haven't ridden one of these things since I was a teenager," Joe mused, stroking his chin. "But I've gotta believe these bikes would get us where we're going a hell of a lot faster than that wheelchair contraption we've been using

Jojo nodded. "I think you're right. I actually got some motorcycle training from one of my battle buddies when I was in the Army. It wasn't much, just the basics, but I think I can handle riding one of these no problem."

"So, we're agreed then?" Joe asked, looking around at the group. "This is our new mode of transportation for the time being?"

"Sounds good to me," Jojo replied. "Let me guess, Maria rides with you while Gram holds onto me?" He chuckled wryly at their current seating arrangements.

"Ha, that works for me, smartass," Joe shot back good-naturedly. He turned to Toni and Maria. "Ladies, are you alright with this plan of action?"

Toni spoke up first. "As long as Jojo here avoids crater-sized potholes, I'll hang on for dear life. Sure, beats walking on these tired old feet, I'll tell you that much."

Joe smiled and looked expectantly at Maria.

"Well, it certainly provides a good opportunity to get...closer," she said, slightly embarrassed. "I'm game if you are." A hint of a smile played on her lips.

"Then it's settled!" Joe said. "My lady, your chariot awaits. Alright everyone, mount up!"

After scavenging the extra supplies from the bodies, the group paired off to claim their bikes. Joe swung his leg over the Harley and felt it rumble to life between his thighs. The sensation sparked nostalgia of his long-past youth. Maria slid on behind him and wrapped her arms around his waist. Her touch made his heart skip a beat.

Jojo and Toni situated themselves on the second motorcycle, a smaller Honda model. Within minutes they were off, cruising down the open highway at speeds unfathomable just hours earlier. The wind whipped Joe's hair as Maria gripped him tightly. He couldn't help but enjoy her closeness and started to daydream about their potential future together.

Unknown to Joe, Maria was also savoring their newfound intimacy. With her cheek pressed against his back and her fingers laced around his abdomen, she felt a growing desire for an emotional and physical connection. The motorcycle had brought them closer in more ways than one.

CHAPTER SIXTEEN
TWO TRAVELERS

Paulette trudged along the deserted highway, her sturdy walking shoes kicking up small clouds of dust with each weary step. Worry clouded her mind as she thought of her children, so many miles away. Would Joe and Jojo make it out of Miami safely? She hoped their survival skills would see them through. But her heart ached for Taylor, Jake and little Parker. Her stubborn daughter would likely refuse to leave the city, putting her family at risk.

Paulette estimated she had at least a hundred and fifty miles to cover before reaching Joe's cabin near Lake Harris. If she could manage ten miles a day, it would take a couple of weeks, maybe longer. She steeled her resolve and pushed on through the heat and isolation. This journey would test her stamina, but Paulette refused to dwell on the challenges ahead.

Rounding a bend, Paulette spotted a lone figure sitting beneath a gnarled oak tree. Drawing nearer, she saw it was a teenage girl, head buried in her arms. The girl's clothes were dirty and torn, her dark tangled hair obscuring her face. Paulette hesitated then called out gently so as not to startle her.

"Hello? Are you okay?"

The girl's head jerked up; eyes wide with alarm. She scrambled to her feet but stayed rooted in place as if poised to flee. Paulette held up her hands in a calming gesture.

"It's alright, I'm not going to hurt you. My name's Paulette. What's your name?"

The girl hesitated, then replied warily. "Alicia."

"That's a lovely name," Paulette said. "You look like you could use some help. Is everything okay?"

Alicia dropped her gaze. "I ain't got nowhere to go. My family's all gone."

Paulette's heart went out to this lost girl who reminded her so much of her own daughter Taylor. On impulse, she made a choice.

"Why don't you come with me? I could use the company, and I have a place we can go where you'll be safe.

Alicia looked searchingly at Paulette, and Paulette thought she saw a spark of hope amidst the fear and mistrust in the girl's eyes.

"You'd do that for me?" Alicia asked uncertainly. At Paulette's reassuring nod, she slowly stepped forward.

"Well, okay then. Thank you kindly."

Paulette smiled warmly and gestured for Alicia to walk with her. As they journeyed on together, Alicia began to open up bit by bit, sharing parts of her painful past. In turn, Paulette talked of her worries for her family, grateful for Alicia's listening ear. By the day's end, they made camp in companionable silence, both taking comfort in having a travel partner on this bleak trek.

In the morning, Paulette awoke with renewed purpose, feeling closer to her goal of reaching Joe's cabin. Alicia too seemed less haunted after a night of dreamless sleep; her defenses lowered. They packed up camp and continued north, their spirits buoyed by a growing sense of kinship.

Over the miles, their bond deepened. Paulette was reminded of her younger self in Alicia's quiet courage, while Alicia came to see Paulette as the mother she had lost too soon. Each found strength in the other as the days passed in a steady plodding rhythm.

Somehow, in this harsh new world, their paths

had intersected. And now, united in fledgling hope, the two travelers moved forward through the badlands, the cabin drawing nearer day by weary day.

CHAPTER SEVENTEEN
SCAVENGING FOR SUPPLIES

The smell of smoke grew stronger as Jake, Taylor, Parker and Claire approached the outskirts of Bunnell. Up ahead, plumes of dark smoke billowed up from the town center.

Jake's jaw tightened. "Something's burning. Could mean trouble."

Taylor shifted little Parker higher on her hip. The toddler babbled happily, oblivious to the adults' tension. "Let's go around. Avoid the town if we can."

Claire nodded, face grim. "We'll skirt the perimeter. Stay hidden in the trees."

They moved cautiously through the woods, parallel to the lonely back roads leading into town. Before long, an abandoned gas station appeared through the foliage.

Jake hesitated. "We could check inside. Might find supplies."

"I'll go," Claire said firmly. "You three wait here." Taylor opened her mouth to protest but Claire was already slipping through the trees toward the building. She let out a frustrated huff.

Jake's eyes followed Claire's progress. "We've got her back if anything happens," he assured his wife.

They hunkered down, alert and uneasy as they kept watch outside the station. After a few tense minutes, Claire reappeared, clutching a few scavenged items.

"Got some water and chips—" she started to say when a scraggly man burst from the bushes and grabbed her hair.

Taylor stifled a scream. Adrenaline flooding his system, Jake didn't hesitate. In two quick strides he was upon the man, pistol-whipping him hard across the back of the skull.

The man crumpled. Jake pulled a shaking Claire away from his limp form.

"You, okay?" Jake asked urgently.

Claire nodded, face pale. Taylor joined them, cooing soothingly to a confused Parker.

"Let's see what you found," Taylor said, hoping to redirect Claire's focus.

Claire managed a shaky smile, revealing the

bottles of water and a small bag of chips.

"Salt and vinegar!" Taylor noted with a forced cheer. "My favorite."

After quickly stashing their scavenged goods, the group hurried on, shaken by the close call. Claire's eyes were haunted but determined as she pressed forward. Parker babbled happily in Taylor's arms, blissfully unaware of the dangers around her. Jake kept his pistol loose in his hand as they moved deeper into the woods, his youthful features hardened by grim experience.

The smoke from Bunnell trailed them for miles, a stark reminder of the lawless world Parker was being raised in. Jake and Taylor locked eyes, silently vowing to shield their daughter from such darkness, whatever the cost.

CHAPTER EIGHTEEN
TENSE TOWNS

The rumble of the motorcycles pierced the quiet countryside as Joe and the others sped down the empty road. With her arms wrapped snugly around Joe's waist, Maria clung to him, her body pressed close against his back. Though her warmth was a welcome comfort, Joe had to keep his mind focused on the potential dangers ahead rather than being distracted by her touch.

They were getting close now, nearing the outskirts of South Bay, the first small town on this leg of their journey. With a population of less than five thousand, South Bay wasn't huge, but Joe knew even one malicious person lurking about could spell trouble. He tensed, gripping the handlebars tightly as they coasted into the town limits.

Beside him, Jojo's gaze continuously scanned the storefronts, houses, and side streets they passed. His muscles were taut, prepared to react to the first sign of a threat. Toni sat rigidly on the seat behind Jojo, bracing herself against the jostling of the motorcycle. Though the ride was rough on her aging body, she ground her teeth and endured the discomfort without complaint.

Their engines thundered as they rolled cautiously down South Bay's main street, announcing their presence. But the town appeared lifeless, empty. Not a soul stirred as they rumbled through the central intersection and continued on up the road, the buildings soon giving way again to stretches of farmland.

Joe breathed a quiet sigh of relief as the last building receded behind them. They had made it through South Bay without incident. Now only Clewiston lay between them and the next long, open stretch of road. Joe prayed they could bypass the town just as smoothly.

Glancing down, he noticed the gas gauge hovering just above empty. The motorcycle was nearly out of fuel. How much longer could they keep up this pace before the tank ran dry? At least the bikes had gotten them this far in a fraction of the time, shaving several days off their grueling journey.

Maria nestled against Joe's back, jolting a bit as

the motorcycle bounced over a rough patch of road. Jojo kept pace, his eyes alert for any sign of danger or trouble as Clewiston's outskirts came into view up ahead. They were nearly through this leg of their difficult trek, thanks to the mobility the motorcycles provided. But Joe knew the hardest parts still lay before them on the long road ahead.

The engines roared as they raced towards Clewiston, focused now on their destination. Just a little further and they would be through this town too. The motorcycles sped on up the road kicking up plumes of dust in their wake, carrying them onwards into the next stage of their perilous journey.

CHAPTER NINETEEN
RUNNING ON EMPTY

Jojo slowed his motorcycle as his father signaled for them to pull over. He expertly guided the bike to the gravel shoulder of the lonely rural road they had been traveling on since leaving Clewiston. When he came to a stop, he put down the kickstand and swung his leg over the seat.

Joe brought his motorcycle to a halt behind his son's and killed the engine. He gingerly dismounted, his joints protesting after the long, jarring ride.

"Getting too old for this crap," Joe muttered, stretching his back. He shook his head and joined Jojo, who had walked back to check on Toni and Maria.

"How y'all holding up back there?" Jojo asked with concern. The two women looked weary and covered in road dust but nodded that they were okay.

"Just ready to take a load off my aching back,"

Toni replied with a wan smile. At 80 years old, the continuous days of hard travel had taken their toll.

Maria patted her knee reassuringly. "We'll rest soon. This old girl's tougher than she looks."

Toni snorted but gave Maria's hand an affectionate squeeze. The two women had grown close during their shared ordeal.

Joe stood with his hands on his hips, surveying their surroundings. They were surrounded by open pastureland dotted with palm trees. In the distance, a few isolated homes could be seen. But no signs of life stirred.

"So, what's the plan, Dad?" Jojo asked, coming up beside him. At 33, he still towered over his father by several inches. But Joe's natural air of authority meant Jojo still deferred to him as leader of their family band.

"We need to talk, gas," Joe said grimly. "By my reckoning' we've both only got about a quarter tank left. We ain't gonna get far on fumes."

Jojo nodded thoughtfully, his brow furrowing. "Yeah, I was wondering about that. My gauge is dipping low too."

"I figure our best bet is to try siphoning from some of these abandoned cars we've been passing," Joe said. "Problem is, we ain't got anything to siphon with."

Jojo's eyes lit up. "That's a great idea! If we can find a hose, we could scavenge gas and keep moving."

"Exactly," Joe said. "Only question is where are we gonna find a hose, way out here?"

He quickly explained the plan to Toni and Maria. "We gotta find a way to siphon gas from other vehicles before we're totally dry. Y'all know where we might find something to use as a hose?"

Maria tapped her finger against her chin thoughtfully before suggesting, "How about one of these houses nearby? Many folks have hoses for gardening we could use."

"Good thinking," Joe said. "Okay, here's the plan. Jojo, take your bike since you've got more gas and scout those homes for a hose. The rest of us will stay put and conserve what little fuel we've got left."

"You got it, Dad," Jojo said, striding back to his motorcycle. He straddled the bike, turned the ignition, and sped off down the road in a plume of dust.

Jojo slowed to a crawl as he approached the first isolated home set back from the road. It was a single-story stucco house that looked long abandoned, its yard overgrown with weeds. But there by the corner he spotted a coiled green garden hose.

"Bingo," Jojo muttered, killing the engine and rolling to a stop. He swung his leg over and cautiously approached the house, one hand hovering over the pistol on his hip. The place looked empty, but he had learned the hard way not to take chances.

When he drew nearer, the movement at the corner of his eye made him spin around, gun drawn. But it was just a torn curtain fluttering through a broken window. Jojo shook his head, laughing nervously at his jumpiness.

He made it to the spigot and grabbed the hose. As he began unraveling it, a shotgun blast rang out. Jojo dove for cover as buckshot peppered the side of the house inches from where he stood.

"Dammit!" He sprinted for his motorcycle, ducking low as another deafening blast sent splinters flying around him. He fired up the engine and peeled away, fishtailing on the gravel road.

Breathing hard, Jojo slowed and looked back. No one emerged from the house in pursuit. But they sure as hell made their point clear about trespassers.

Jaw set, Jojo continued on. He'd be damned if he went back empty-handed after all that. The next place looked deserted too - a small cottage set off a dirt driveway. Jojo killed the engine out of earshot and pushed his bike up the drive.

Sure enough, a green hose lay coiled up beneath a spigot around back. Keeping a sharp eye out, Jojo wrestled to unscrew the rigid hose from the valve. With a grunt, it finally gave way, and he stumbled back, hose in hand. Quickly he coiled it and tied it to his bike. Wasting no time, he hopped on and roared back to the others.

Joe spotted Jojo's returning figure appearing as a dust cloud on the horizon. As he drew nearer, Joe's brow furrowed seeing the hose tied to his bike. His son was one stubborn SOB, he thought with a shake of his head.

"Mission accomplished," Jojo declared, braking to a stop. "But not without some unfriendly fire. Guess they didn't take too kindly to me borrowing their hose."

Despite his concern, Joe couldn't help but swell with pride. "That's my boy," he said, clapping a hand on Jojo's shoulder. Jojo grinned, holding up the hose like a trophy. It wasn't the homecoming he expected, but his dad's praise meant the world.

Let's cut this thing down to a more manageable size."

Maria reached into her bag of supplies pulling out the knife she had plunged into the neck of the biker who had threatened them previously. She shuddered at the memory.

"Here ya go Joe, this should work."

As Joe sized up the knife he said, "Perfect, thanks Maria, this will do nicely."

Joe and Jojo make quick work of cutting the hose into a shorter version that would be easier to travel with and still long enough that would give them plenty of length for the main task it was needed for. They thought it best to have more than one and cut several lengths of hose and attached them to the bikes. "Never hurts to have spares." Jojo said. "One is good, but two or more is better, and God forbid if we should ever get separated it's good, we have a couple of these on each bike."

"You're absolutely right, great thinking Jojo." Joe said, patting his son on the back. "Now let's gas up these bikes and get the hell outta here before our luck runs out."

Together they got to work siphoning precious fuel from cars along the route, the hose working like a charm. Maria and Toni cheered them on, optimistic once again now that the motorcycles could keep eating up miles toward their destination.

With bikes topped off and supplies secured, the group was soon back in the saddle cruising down the empty backroads of rural Florida. Jojo took up the rear this time, keeping a watchful eye out behind them for any sign of pursuit. But the road stayed empty, only the sound of motors and wind in their ears. Up ahead, Joe navigated assuredly based on his knowledge of the area.

And so, they traveled on, the foursome now bound by their shared adversities and common purpose. Each mile brought them closer to the haven they dreamed of and farther from the chaos they left behind. As the sun began to dip towards the horizon, Joe knew they still had far to go. But with his family beside him and gas in their bikes, he was confident they would make it. Tonight, he thought they would sleep easy knowing their escape was working and hope remained.

CHAPTER TWENTY
HAPPIER TIMES

The miles clicked by as they sped ahead past Moore Haven, but darkness was falling, and they needed to find a place to sleep for the night. Joe kept his eyes peeled to the side of the road, searching for somewhere they could stop and make camp.

As they drove, Joe spotted a road sign. "Well, I'll be damned." Joe thought to himself. The sign read Fisheating Creek five miles ahead.

The sign jogged something in Joe's memory. He suddenly remembered a camping trip from his youth. His first ever camping trip. Shortly after graduating high school.

He and three of his high school buddies on a complete whim had made the trip to Fisheating Creek to camp and fish for a weekend. None of them knew the first thing about camping.

Joe chuckled internally as he recalled that

miserable trip. The four of them had made the trip with only one small two-person tent, which ended up crooked and lopsided.

They'd brought some ground beef to make hamburgers, but never thought to bring an actual cooking surface to use over an open campfire.

One of the guys seemed to recall something called silver dollars. You form a hamburger patty and wrap it in aluminum foil and then throw it into the fire.

Joe remembered trying to get the "Silver Dollars" out of the fire and opening them up only to find some very charred burgers. The meal was certainly far from gourmet.

Then with only one tent, two of the guys took that While Joe and another friend slept in the car.

The mosquitoes at Fisheating Creek in the summer are vicious. You had a choice. Be eaten alive or roll up the windows and roast.

As uncomfortable as it was, that weekend at Fisheating Creek had lodged itself firmly in Joe's memory. The four friends had laughed until their sides ached at their incompetence. It was one of those unforgettable times that you look back on fondly.

Now, years later, Joe knew exactly where they would spend the night.

CHAPTER TWENTY ONE
SANCTUARY FOUND

As the campground entrance came into view, Joe signaled for Jojo to slow down and follow his lead. He turned into the long dirt driveway, his headlights cutting through the darkness to reveal the small camp store and clusters of vacant campsites. Being remote and secluded, the campground appeared untouched by the chaos they'd left behind.

Joe pulled up alongside the camp store and dismounted. Turning to Jojo, "We need to get inside and see if there are any supplies we can use for the night and the rest of the trip. Flashlights, bedrolls, non-perishable food—anything useful. Hopefully this place hasn't been completely cleaned out."

Jojo nodded; his expression serious. "I'm on it."

The women also quickly got off the motorcycles while Jojo and Joe approached the store entrance. Jojo smashed the glass door panel with the butt of his rifle and reached through to unlock it. Stepping inside, the beam of his flashlight revealed shelves still well-stocked with equipment.

"Jackpot," Jojo said. "Doesn't look like anyone's touched this place. Grab some carts and let's load up."

Soon they were wheeling cartloads of supplies outside: tents, sleeping bags, mess kits, camping stoves, propane cylinders, bottles of water, flashlights with extra batteries — anything they could use to improve their chances on the road. Toni and Maria helped unload it all and start sorting through everything.

By the time Joe and Jojo had finished ransacking the store, full darkness had descended. The moon glowed faintly behind a veil of clouds. Using a hatchet from the store, Joe chopped dead branches from surrounding trees while Jojo kindled a fire in the stone-lined campfire pit. Soon orange flames licked upward, crackling and sparking.

The group worked quietly but efficiently together to set up tents and roll out sleeping bags. Maria and Toni prepared a simple hot meal over the fire using canned stew from the store. The salty, savory smell of the bubbling stew made Joe's mouth water. It would be their first hot meal in several days.

When it was ready, they sat together around the flickering firelight, steaming metal bowls warming their hands. The dancing fire lit their faces in a warm glow as they ate hungrily. Above, the stars peeked intermittently between the clouds. A gentle wind rustled the trees surrounding their camp. For the first time in days, some of the stress and tension began to ease from the group's shoulders. Bellies full, weariness setting in, they began to relax into an unexpected moment of refuge on their arduous journey.

CHAPTER TWENTY TWO
RIVERSIDE RESPITE

J oe gazed thoughtfully out at the familiar campground, a wave of nostalgia washing over him.

"I know this sounds crazy," he said, turning to address the group, "and I know we're in a hurry to get to the cabin, but may I make a suggestion?"

"What's on your mind, Pops?" Jojo replied, leaning forward with interest.

Joe rubbed his chin, looking pensive in the dusky light. "Well, maybe it's the nostalgia of this place, or maybe I'm just going crazy, but it seems we've found a bit of a safe haven here. At least for the moment. And I think we could all use a break to recharge our batteries around a nice campfire. I guess what I'm saying is, maybe we could slow down a bit and stay here tonight and tomorrow and leave the next day. Is that crazy?"

Maria chimed in eagerly. "Joe, I think that's a

great idea! I know I'm exhausted, and the fire would feel so cozy. I'm sure your mom could use some rest too. We all could." She gestured enthusiastically. "This place, at least for now, seems like a safe place."

Toni nodded her agreement, face glowing in the campfire's light. "I think a day of rest would do us all good. I'm with you on it, Joe.

Jojo leaned back, nodding as well. "Yeah, Pops, I can't disagree. We could definitely all use a break."

Joe's face relaxed into a smile, the creases in his weathered face smoothing out. "Then we're in agreement. Let's unwind a bit here while we have the chance."

Soon a cheery blaze crackled, the orange flames illuminating their faces as dusk settled over the quiet campground. They sat in a circle around the fire, grateful for its warmth and light. For the first time in days, a collective sense of relief washed over the group. Out here, away from the chaos and uncertainty, they could almost pretend things were normal.

CHAPTER TWENTY THREE
SPARKS IN THE DARK

T oni yawned as she stood up from the log around the campfire. "Well, I think I'm going to turn in for the night. These old bones need some rest."

She headed towards one of the tents they had found earlier in the camp store. At 80 years old, Toni tired easily, though she remained determined to keep up.

Jojo also stood up, rubbing his eyes. "Yeah, I'm beat too. It's been a long couple of days."

He followed Toni and disappeared into the tent beside hers.

This left Joe and Maria sitting alone together around the crackling fire, the dancing flames illuminating their faces in the growing darkness. Both felt suddenly nervous being alone together for the first time. The attraction between them had been steadily building, and now the sexual tension was palpable.

They made some brief small talk at first, stealing furtive glances at each other when they thought the other wasn't looking. Joe felt his pulse quickening as he admired Maria's petite, curvy figure bathed in the firelight. Her warm brown eyes seemed to sparkle as she laughed at his lame attempts at jokes.

A silence fell between them, the only sound the snapping and popping of the logs burning in the pit. Joe's mind raced as he tried to think of something charming or witty to say to break the tension.

Maria spoke up first. "So... come here often?" she joked with a playful grin.

Joe laughed, the sound seeming loud in the stillness of the night. Her wit and easygoing nature never failed to delight him.

"As a matter of fact, I do," he replied. "There's no better place to wine and dine a beautiful woman than a musty old campground in the middle of nowhere."

Maria's cheeks flushed at the subtle compliment. "Why Mr. Kelly, are you flirting with me?"

"Maybe just a little," Joe admitted with a roguish smile.

Their banter continued, growing more flirtatious as the lingering glances became longer and more daring. Joe kept waiting for Maria to rebuff his advances or change the subject, but to his pleasant surprise, she seemed to welcome them.

Emboldened, he shifted closer to her on the log until their thighs were nearly touching. He heard Maria's breath hitch, but she held his gaze steadily, a hint of longing in her dark eyes.

Without thinking, Joe reached out to brush a stray lock of hair back from her face, letting his fingers linger to caress her cheek. Her skin was soft and warm beneath his touch.

Maria tensed slightly at first but soon relaxed, tilting her head and leaning into his palm with a shy smile. Her reaction sent Joe's pulse racing.

Heart pounding, he began slowly leaning in, their faces drawing closer. He paused just inches from her lips, close enough to feel her quickened breath against his mouth. At the last moment, he diverted and placed a gentle kiss on her forehead instead.

Maria let out a soft, disappointed sigh at the loss of contact but felt a secret thrill at his chivalry.

As much as she ached for more, she knew it was too soon.

"It's getting late," Joe murmured, his voice husky. "We should probably call it a night before this goes any further."

Maria nodded reluctantly. "You're probably right." As stimulating as their flirtation had been, she was grateful Joe hadn't tried to rush things. It showed how much he respected her.

They exchanged goodnights, both flushed and jittery as they retreated to their separate tents.

Joe ducked into the small, musty canvas shelter, his pulse still racing as he replayed the heated moments at the fire. He had never desired someone so strongly, at least not since his ex-wife Paulette decades ago. The intensity of his attraction to Maria after such a short time surprised and exhilarated him.

As he settled onto the creaky cot, Joe smiled to himself, feeling more alive than he had in years. Getting to know Maria these past few days had awakened something in him he thought was lost forever. For the first time since the EMP, the future seemed to hold promise and hope instead of just hardship and survival. He only prayed that Maria felt the same way. Joe eventually drifted off, dreaming of soft lips and molten brown eyes.

In the tent beside him, Maria lay awake for hours, her body humming from the exhilaration of being so close to Joe. The gentle caress of his fingers still lingered like a phantom touch on her skin. She pressed her fingertips to the spot on her forehead where his lips had grazed, cherishing the intimacy of that fleeting contact.

Thoughts of Joe filled her mind as she replayed their flirtatious exchange over the fire. She had seen the desire burning in his slate gray eyes as the space between them shrank. And she knew her own longing was just as evident.

When he had kissed her forehead so tenderly, it took all her willpower not to draw him into a real kiss. But they had only just met, and Maria didn't want to rush things. She was grateful Joe was gentleman enough not to assume more than she was ready for.

Still, the potent attraction between them was undeniable. As she finally drifted off, Maria wondered what the next days would bring and if she dared open her heart again after so much loss. For now, she would take it one moment at a time and see where this unexpected connection led.

The next morning, Joe emerged from his tent feeling refreshed but anxious to see Maria again. The memory of their charged encounter the night before still gripped him. He wondered if things would be awkward between them in the harsh light of day or if the spark of passion still burned.

He didn't have to wait long to find out. Maria soon exited her own tent looking well-rested. When she caught sight of Joe across the way, her face lit up with an effervescent smile.

"Good morning," she said warmly, walking over to him.

"Morning," Joe replied, unable to keep a grin from spreading across his weathered face. Her cheerful demeanor instantly put him at ease. Things didn't seem awkward at all. If anything, there was now an added layer of intimacy and unspoken understanding between them.

"Sleep, okay?" he asked.

Maria nodded. "Surprisingly, yes. Those cots aren't too bad once you get used to the creaking."

"It beats sleeping on the ground, that's for sure," Joe chuckled in agreement.

Their conversation flowed easily as Joe prepared a simple breakfast of rehydrated scrambled eggs and they discussed plans for the day. Soon the others began to exit their tents and join them around the campfire.

Toni seemed well-rested and remarked on how comfortable the cots were compared to some of the beds she'd slept on over the years. Jojo stretched and yawned, not fully awake yet but ready to take on the day's work ahead.

As the group talked and ate, Joe and Maria's eyes continually drifted back to one another, their secretive smiles conveying the new closeness between them. Both looked forward to finding more chances to be alone as the day went on.

CHAPTER TWENTY FOUR
SEEING THROUGH HER EYES

Paulette and Alicia walked slowly through the dense forest, picking their way carefully over fallen branches and around thickets of brambles. The morning sun filtered down through the canopy of leaves above them, dappling the ground with patches of light.

Paulette asked Alicia how she came to be alone on the road. Alicia letting out a deep sigh explained that her father was shot a few days ago by several men that were looting a store.

"It was so senseless." She explained. "They came out of the store and saw my dad and I walking past the store and just started firing, dad was hit and fell to ground, and the men ran off."

Alicia continued, "He was gone, there was nothing I could do, I - I didn't even have a chance to say goodbye." She said as her eyes began to fill with tears.

I'm so sorry Alicia, that is awful and I'm so sorry you had to go through that" Paulette said soothingly.

Paulette asked, "And what about your mom, where is she?"

Alicia, reflecting back on her childhood said, "I was young when mom left, barely eight years old. One day mom was there, the next she was just... gone. My father told me she had run off with another man, it was a tough pill to swallow that's for sure."

She continued, "I still remember waiting day after day on the front porch of our little house, hoping each car that turned down our street might be my mother, finally coming back home. But she never did. For a long time, I even blamed myself, I had always wondered if I had done something wrong, something to drive my mom away. The guilt ate away at me for years, but now I know it was nothing I had done, it was her own selfishness. Anyway, I never saw her again."

Alicia went on reminiscing while Paulette became strangely silent.

"Dad did his best after mom left, raising a daughter all on his own. Thinking back now, it had to have been just as tough on him as it was for me. It's hard growing up as a young girl without a mother's guidance. I remember when I first started developing these things." Pointing to her breasts. "It was, let's just say, uncomfortable trying to talk to my father about things like buying my first bra."

Alicia chuckled now. "I remember the day I actually got up the nerve to broach the subject with him. Dads' eyes nearly popped out of his head." She giggles. "He was so flustered, he raced out to the store to pick out training bras for me. He came home with a huge shopping bag filled with bras of all sizes and styles. It was awkward to say the least, but also very sweet at the same time, you know."

Alicia goes on. "Getting my first period was even worse. I was terrified, I started bleeding, and I had no idea what was going on. I ran to dad crying. He told me everything would be alright and that this was a natural thing that happens to all young women. He made me feel so much better. Next thing I know he scrambled to educate himself, picking up pamphlets from the drugstore and gathering all the feminine hygiene products he could find. I basically had my own drugstore in my bathroom."

She chuckles as she remembers. "He bought everything, I had tampons in small, medium and large, pads in every size, with wings, without wings. You name it Dad got it. God bless him, he did his best, but a young girl really needs a mother at those times."

Beside her, Paulette suddenly let out a strangled sob. Alicia turned to her in surprise.

"What's wrong?" she asked with concern. "Are you okay?"

But Paulette seemed unable to speak, overcome with emotion as tears ran down her cheeks. She struggled to compose herself. Alicia waited patiently for her to be ready to talk.

Finally, in a choked voice, Paulette explained haltingly that Alicia's story had brought back painful memories of her own past mistakes.

To Alicia's shock, Paulette confessed that years ago, when her own daughter Taylor was around eight years old, Paulette had left her family for another man. She had abandoned her children, just as Alicia's mother had done.

The revelation stunned Alicia. She never would have imagined that Paulette's past paralleled her own mother's actions so closely.

Paulette described through her tears how she had left Miami to move to Punta Gorda with her new boyfriend, rarely bothering to visit or spend much time with her children after that. It had been the biggest mistake of her life; one she had regretted every day since. The guilt and shame of what she had done haunted her constantly. Leaving her kids had created wounds that never fully healed.

As Alicia listened, she saw Paulette in a new light, realizing the depth of remorse the other woman felt over her actions. Impulsively, she reached out and put a comforting hand on Paulette's shoulder.

"I'm so sorry," Paulette said, trying to compose herself and wiping her eyes. "Telling me about your own mother just brought back a lot of memories for me. It made me see things through the eyes of my own daughter and what she must have gone through. I didn't mean to break down like that."

"It's okay, I understand," Alicia said gently. "We all make mistakes in life. I don't judge you for what happened in the past."

Paulette looked at her with gratitude through her tears. "You're very kind not to condemn me," she said. "You remind me so much of my little girl." Her voice broke again on those words. "I'd give anything to be able to go back and make different choices. To undo the pain, I caused them."

Alicia gave her shoulder a comforting squeeze. "Maybe this situation is giving you a chance to start making amends," she suggested. "We're on our way to see your family again at the cabin. It could be an opportunity for reconciliation."

Paulette dried her eyes, considering this. "You're

right," she said finally. "I'm going to do my best to try and repair things with my children, as much as I can. I know they may not ever be able to forgive me completely. But I have to try."

The two women continued their walk through the forest.

After seeing Paulette's raw remorse over her past mistakes, Alicia felt a sense of compassion for her. On impulse, she reached out and took the older woman's hand in her own, giving it a gentle, supportive squeeze. Paulette grasped her hand tightly, drawing comfort from the contact.

For the first time, Paulette felt a sense of hope about the impending reunion with her family. With Alicia by her side, she felt ready to face them again.

CHAPTER TWENTY FIVE
BURDENS OF THE PAST

The morning sun filtered through the trees, casting flickering shadows on the worn forest path. Jake walked in silence, his eyes downcast and shoulders slumped. Taylor and Claire exchanged worried glances as they followed several paces behind.

Ever since the violent encounter with the marauders two days prior, Jake had been unusually quiet and withdrawn. At first Taylor and Claire had given him space, understanding he was grappling with the trauma of taking lives to protect Claire. But now his somber demeanor was starting to concern them.

When they reached a small creek, Claire suggested they refill their water bottles and take a short break.

Gratefully lowering her pack, Taylor seized the opportunity to check on her husband.

"Jake?" she asked gently, placing a hand on his arm. "Is everything okay?"

He lifted his head slowly, his eyes glistening with unshed tears. "No, not really," he admitted.

Taylor's brow furrowed in sympathy.

Claire hovered nearby, unsure whether to stay or give them privacy. But Jake's next words rooted her to the spot.

"I killed two men, Taylor. And beat another so badly he probably died too. I never thought myself capable of that kind of violence, but I did it without hesitation." His voice broke. "What's happening to me?"

Taylor enveloped him in a fierce hug. "You were protecting us. You had no choice."

Over Taylor's shoulder, Jake met Claire's earnest gaze. "I'm sorry you had to see that side of me."

Claire stepped forward and squeezed his hand. "There's nothing to apologize for. You saved my life." She swallowed hard. "Those men would have..." Her voice trailed off, the unspoken words hanging heavy between them.

Jake shook his head. "That's just it. The killing itself doesn't bother me. I feel no remorse or guilt over what I did. Only..." He hesitated, struggling to articulate the disturbing emotions swirling within him.

"Only what?" Taylor prodded gently.

"Only that the act of killing didn't affect me more. I ended three lives and felt nothing. No hesitation, no regret, no sadness." Jake raked a hand through his hair in agitation.

"What kind of person does that make me? Shouldn't I be haunted by this?" His voice dropped to a tortured whisper. "What if I'm turning into a monster?"

The anguish and self-loathing in Jake's eyes pierced Taylor's heart. She threw her arms around him, tears sliding down her cheeks.

"You listen to me, Jake Green. You are the furthest thing from a monster. You're a good, kind, gentle man trying to survive in a brutal world."

Taylor held him at arm's length, her expression fierce. "If you hadn't done what you did, Claire and I wouldn't be standing here right now, not to mention your little girl, Parker. Those men would have done unspeakable things to us."

Claire laid a supportive hand on Jake's shoulder. "Taylor's right. You're a hero in my book." She offered him a small smile. "I know you, Jake. This wasn't murder. It was self-defense - you protected your family."

Jake scrubbed a hand over his face. "I want to

believe that. I wish I could see it as clearly as you both do. I took lives and it didn't impact me - that scares me more than the act itself."

He shook his head as if trying to jar his thoughts into place. "I appreciate you both trying to help me process this. Maybe with time..." His voice drifted off.

Taylor and Claire exchanged a worried look. A somber silence descended over the trio as they finished refilling their bottles. But before they moved to gather their packs, Claire and Taylor both wrapped Jake in a fierce embrace.

"We're here for you," Claire murmured. "You don't have to carry this alone." Taylor nodded her fervent agreement.

Jake offered them a faint smile. "I know. Thank you." He gestured towards the path ahead. "We should keep moving. Still a way to go before we reach your dad's cabin."

They fell into step behind Jake, keeping a watchful eye on him. Though he carried himself a bit straighter now, there was a shadow behind his eyes that hadn't been there before. A darkness seeded by the cruel necessities of this lawless new world.

That evening they bunked down in an abandoned barn, the broken-down tractor and scattered tools evidence it had once been part of a working farm.

Claire tried to make Jake as comfortable as possible, offering him the lone mattress and extra blanket she'd scavenged from the farmhouse.

But as she drifted off to sleep on the hard-packed dirt floor, Claire heard the low murmur of Jake and Taylor's hushed voices on the other side of the barn. She strained to listen to their conversation while feigning sleep.

"I'm worried about you, Jake," came Taylor's anxious whisper. "It's not like you to be so troubled."

Claire heard Jake sigh heavily. "I can't shake this numbness, Taylor. Ever since that day I have felt... detached. Like I'm watching myself from far away."

"You went through a trauma. Your mind is just trying to process..."

"It's more than that," Jake interrupted. "It's like a part of my soul died with those men. I ended lives and felt nothing. What kind of person can do that?" His voice broke on the last word.

Taylor was silent for a long moment. "Jake, listen to me," she finally said, an edge creeping into her tone. "You are not defined by one act of violence. You did what you had to do in order to protect the people you love."

Claire could imagine Taylor gripping his face,

forcing him to meet her fierce gaze. "You are kind. You are good. You are loving. Don't let this world twist you into believing otherwise."

Jake exhaled a shaky breath. "You always see the best in me, Taylor."

"Because it's there. You've just lost sight of it." Her voice radiated absolute conviction. "I know your heart, Jake Green. And it is good."

Wrapped in her bedroll, Claire allowed herself a small smile. Taylor's steadfast faith seemed to be getting through to Jake, lifting the cloud of despair that had been following him since that horrific day.

Maybe with Taylor's help Jake would find a way to forgive himself. To understand he wasn't defined by violence, but by the compassion that led him to commit it - sacrificing a piece of his soul to protect those he loved.

Reassured, Claire let the rise and fall of Jake and Taylor's murmured voices lull her into a dreamless sleep.

CHAPTER TWENTY SIX
FISHING FOR LOVE

Joe, Jojo, Toni and Maria sat around the smoldering fire pit, sipping instant coffee from chipped enamel mugs. The four of them were quiet, gazing thoughtfully at the wisps of smoke twisting up into the blue sky. It was a peaceful moment, one they all secretly cherished, knowing such tranquility was fleeting in their ragged new world.

Jojo broke the silence first, setting his mug on the ground with a dull clunk. "So, Pops, what's the plan for today?" he asked Joe. "We gonna just sit around this fire all day or actually accomplish something?"

Joe looked up, glancing around at each of them studiously. He rubbed his stubbled chin before replying. "Well, now that you mention it, I did have an idea," he said.

"And what might that be?" Jojo asked, one eyebrow arched.

"The name of this campground is Fish Eating Creek," Joe said. "I thought maybe we might try our hand at actual fish eating. There are canoes down by the bank we can use. And plenty of tackle we grabbed last night in the shop."

Toni scoffed loudly. "Like hell if I'm going fishing or getting in any rickety canoe!" she declared, wisps of silver hair fluttering as she shook her head. "You boys knock yourselves out, but this old gal's staying on dry land."

Maria laughed, her warm brown eyes crinkling at Toni's reaction. "I can't say I've done much fishing before," she said. "But I'd love to learn from an expert like yourself, Joe."

Jojo saw the way his dad perked up at Maria's interest. An idea struck him then. "You know what, that all sounds great," Jojo said. "But maybe you should take Maria out yourself, Pops. I don't want to crowd three people in a tiny canoe. Give you two a chance to really focus on the fishing."

He threw in an exaggerated wink at his father, which was clearly visible to everyone, unable to keep a huge grin off his face. "After all, you know what they say - three's a crowd, Dad."

Maria blushed prettily while Joe shot his son a half-amused, half-exasperated look. "Alright then,

I suppose it'll just be you and me, Maria," Joe said, turning to her. "If you're sure you're up for it, that is."

Maria leapt to her feet eagerly. "I'd love nothing more, Joe," she assured him with an excited smile.

Jojo beamed approvingly at his father as Joe stood and walked over to join Maria. As he passed, Joe gave Jojo a playful smack upside the head. "You little shit," he muttered under his breath, before adding softly, "Thank you, son."

Jojo chuckled while Maria hurried off toward the shoreline, Joe following behind her. Rods in hand, the pair made their way down the grassy slope, sneaking giddy glances at each other.

Watching them vanish out of sight, Jojo couldn't wipe the satisfied grin off his face. He'd noticed a spark between his dad and Maria lately. Maybe a relaxing day fishing together was just what they needed.

Satisfied with his matchmaking skills, Jojo settled back in his chair. He met Toni's knowing gaze across the cooling fire pit. "Yep, three's definitely a crowd," Jojo said with a laugh.

Toni just smirked and sipped her coffee.

Down by the gently rippling creek, Joe steadied the green canoe as Maria climbed in. The small boat rocked slightly on the water as she settled onto the worn wooden seat.

"Just sit tight there in the middle for balance," Joe instructed. He set the two fishing rods carefully inside before pushing them off from the muddy bank with one foot.

The canoe slid smoothly across the glassy water as Joe hopped nimbly aboard. Taking a paddle, he rowed them along at a leisurely pace. Dragonflies and mayflies flitted around them, landing occasionally on the water's surface.

Maria trailed one hand over the side, enjoying the feel of the cool water. "This is so nice," she said with a contented sigh. "So peaceful out here."

"One of the few perks of the world ending, I guess," Joe said wryly. "No crowds to deal with at least."

Maria gave a small laugh. "I appreciate you taking the time to teach me to fish, by the way."

"Happy to do it," Joe replied gruffly. He felt suddenly bashful, in a way he hadn't experienced in years. "Hopefully we can actually catch something edible."

"With an experienced angler like yourself, I'm sure we will," Maria said. She favored him with a warm smile that made his heart unexpectedly flutter.

They soon arrived at a shady bend in the creek, sheltered by overhanging trees. Joe dropped the anchor, securing the canoe in place.

"Alright, looks like a good spot to try our luck," he pronounced. He picked up the two rods and began prepping them with crickets he'd found in the tackle shop, demonstrating to Maria how to properly bait the hook.

"Here, now you try," he said, handing her the rod once he'd finished the first. Their fingers brushed lightly as she took it from him. Joe felt a spark travel up his arm at the contact.

Maria bit her lip in concentration as she carefully pierced the wriggling cricket. "Like that?" she asked proudly, holding up the baited hook.

"Perfect, Maria, you never cease to amaze me" Joe said with an approving nod.

With their lines cast, the two of them sat in contented silence, gazing out at the shimmering water and listening to the bird songs in the trees. Joe snuck frequent glances at Maria's profile, struck as always by her natural beauty.

"You know, Jojo was right earlier," Maria said after a while, turning to look at Joe with a teasing glint in her eye. "This is much nicer without a third wheel tagging along."

Joe harrumphed, feeling his face grow warm. "That boy doesn't know when to keep his mouth shut."

"Oh, I don't know about that," Maria said lightly. "I'd say he has a good sense for these sorts of things."

Before Joe could think of a response, Maria's line suddenly grew taut. "Oh! I think I have something!" she cried.

"Reel it in, keep the line tight," Joe coached, leaning in close to observe her form.

Maria cranked the reel, her rod bending as she fought against the fish below the surface. With a splash, she finally pulled it out of the water - a decent-sized largemouth bass.

"I did it! My first catch!" Maria cheered. Laughing, Joe helped unhook the fish and place it in their bucket.

"Nice work. At this rate you'll put me to shame," Joe said proudly.

"Only thanks to an excellent teacher," Maria replied, smiling at him in a way that made Joe's heart do flip-flops again.

They whiled away the rest of the morning fishing together, catching enough for a hearty dinner. All too soon, Joe found himself reluctantly rowing them back to shore, not yet ready for their idyllic day to end.

As the canoe glided across the shimmering creek, Joe decided to take a chance. "Maria, I just wanted to say, spending this time together has been really special," he began gruffly. "Might be crazy, considering the state of things, but I can't remember the last time I was this happy."

He paused, searching her face for a reaction. Maria said nothing, but her eyes shone as she reached out and gave his hand a gentle squeeze.

And in that moment, Joe felt a spark of something he'd thought lost forever - a stirring of joy, of possibility. Gazing into Maria's warm brown eyes, for the first time in a long while, Joe Kelly dared to hope again.

CHAPTER TWENTY SEVEN
DARK ENCOUNTER

Paulette and Alicia continued walking down the desolate highway. The hot sun beat down on them as they trudged along in silence, both focused on putting one foot in front of the other. Up ahead, Paulette spotted a small gas station just off the road. At first glance it appeared deserted, like most buildings they had come across.

"Hey, look over there!" Alicia suddenly blurted out, breaking the silence. She pointed excitedly towards the side of the gas station. "Are those what I think they are?"

Paulette strained her eyes to see what the young girl was looking at. Her vision wasn't as sharp as it used to be.

"Those look like bicycles!" Alicia exclaimed. "That would make traveling so much easier on our feet."

Paulette could just make out the shapes of bikes

leaning against the building. "Yes, it certainly would," she replied, feeling a surge of hope. The thought of gliding easily down the road instead of this endless trudging was certainly appealing.

Before Paulette could say anything more, Alicia suddenly took off running towards the gas station.

"Alicia, stop!" Paulette called after her. But the girl kept going, consumed with youthful impulsiveness.

Paulette struggled to keep up as Alicia raced ahead. Her old body resisted, and she was quickly out of breath. By the time Paulette finally caught up, Alicia was already at the bikes with a look of bitter disappointment on her face.

Up close, it was clear the bikes were just empty shells. Rotted rubber hung off cracked rims, the tires completely flat and useless. There would be no joyriding today. Paulette placed her hand gently on Alicia's slumped shoulder, sharing in the letdown.

Just then, they heard a rustling from inside the gas station. Paulette's heart jumped as a scruffy-looking man emerged, clutching a shotgun in his hands. His cold eyes sized them up behind a tangled mess of a beard.

"Well, well...what do we have here?" he rasped, flashing a yellow grin. "Two pretty little ladies all by their lonesome."

Paulette pulled Alicia back protectively. "We'll just be on our way, mister," she said, trying to keep her voice from shaking.

The man laughed, an ugly sound like rocks in a tin can. "I don't think so, sweetheart," he sneered. "In fact, I think you two should stick around for a spell. It gets a might lonely out here and I'm in need of some female companionship." He gestured with the shotgun. "Now get inside, both of you."

Paulette hesitated, sizing up whether they could make a run for it. The man seemed to read her mind. "Don't even think about trying to run or you'll get a face full of buckshot," he warned. Resigned, Paulette put a protective arm around Alicia and led her toward the doorway, the man's gun trained on their backs.

Inside, the gas station was dim and dusty, most of the shelves bare. The heavy smell of body odor hung in the air. Paulette's heart thudded as the man forced them toward the back room.

"Alright Mama, you tie up the young one good and tight with that rope over there," the man ordered, keeping the shotgun pointed at Paulette.

Reluctantly, Paulette took the rope and bound Alicia's hands behind her back. She tried to give the girl a reassuring squeeze, but her eyes were wide with fear.

"Make sure those knots are good and tight," the man warned. He stepped behind Alicia and roughly checked her bonds, then did the same with the ropes around her ankles.

Satisfied, the man turned back to Paulette. "You did good, Mama. Now me and you are gonna have us a little fun. I'm gonna save this sweet young thing for dessert." He licked his lips and Paulette felt vomit rise in her throat.

"Please, you don't have to do this," Paulette pleaded desperately. "We won't tell anyone, just let us walk away."

The man cut her off. "Now take off that shirt Mama, nice and slow." He leaned against the wall casually, but the shotgun never wavered from Paulette.

With trembling fingers, Paulette complied, tears welling in her eyes. She saw Alicia watching in horror, helpless to do anything.

"The bra too, Mama," the man ordered. Paulette squeezed her eyes shut and removed her bra, feeling utterly exposed and degraded. She kept her arms crossed over her chest.

"Not bad for an old broad," the man remarked.

"But I bet your daughter over there is nice and perky." His grin turned wolfish. "Now the rest of it, honey. Let's see what you've got."

Sobs escaped Paulette as she stripped off the remainder of her clothes under the man's greedy gaze. When she was fully nude, he slowly circled her, taking in every inch of her bare body. Revulsion and rage churned inside Paulette.

The man picked up a handgun from the counter and set down the shotgun. He gestured for Paulette to turn around. "This ain't gonna hurt one bit Mama," he whispered in her ear as he pressed against her. "In fact, I think you're gonna enjoy it real good."

Paulette clenched her eyes closed as she heard the man fiddling with his pants. Then she felt him thrust into her and she screamed as he took her roughly from behind. She could do nothing but weep as the man had his way, feeling only disgust and fury at being so utterly violated.

Finally, it was over. The man gave one last groan of satisfaction. "Lord almighty, just what I needed Mama! Now it's time for that young filly."

Still sobbing and shaken, Paulette stayed crouched on the floor. The man's fluids dripped down her thighs but all she felt was rage. As the man turned away, still fastening his pants, Paulette's eyes desperately scanned the room. They fell on a tire iron laying just a few feet away.

Moving slowly so as not to draw attention, Paulette edged toward the tire iron while the man was still distracted, his sick desires momentarily spent. Her heart pounded as her fingers closed around the cold metal. This monster had to die.

In one motion, Paulette snatched up the tool, whirled around and swung with all her strength. The iron slammed brutally into the man's skull with a nauseating crunch. Blood sprayed as he collapsed to his knees, but Paulette did not stop. She raised the iron and brought it down again and again and again, bludgeoning the man's head into an unrecognizable mess of bone, brains and gore.

At last, Paulette dropped the tire iron. The man lay still in a spreading pool of blood. Hands still shaking from adrenaline, Paulette looked over at Alicia. The girl had squeezed her eyes shut, but tears still leaked out. Paulette quickly grabbed her clothes and dressed, then rushed to untie the trembling girl.

"It's over," Paulette soothed, holding the sobbing teen. "That monster will never hurt anyone again." They clung to each other, the horror of the encounter sinking in. But they had survived, and now it was time to put more distance between them and this dreadful place.

CHAPTER TWENTY EIGHT
CONFESSIONS

J ojo marveled at the large haul of fish Joe and Maria had caught. "Wow! We'll have a feast tonight with all these," he said.

Joe replied, "Can you clean 'em up for us, son?"

"Absolutely, dad. I'm on it," Jojo said as he gathered the fish and headed to the cleaning station.

Joe hurried over to where Maria was sitting at a picnic table away from the others. He had a serious look on his face that told Maria he wanted to speak privately.

"You got quite the catch today," Joe said, breaking the ice.

"I think we both did quite well," Maria said with a smile.

Joe nodded. "Listen Maria, it's been a long, long time since I've had feelings like this for someone. And frankly, I don't really know where to go from here. But I don't like playing games or beating around the bush. So, I'm just gonna lay my cards on the table. I... uhm...really care about you, Maria."

Before Joe could continue, Maria gently interrupted him. "Joe, I know exactly how you feel. I feel the same way. I'm just as confused and lost about this. I don't know how to move forward either. But I have to be honest, I've had some very strong feelings for you since the moment we met. Feelings I just can't deny."

Maria took a deep breath before continuing. "But if I'm going to be absolutely honest with you, I need to tell you...I'm still a married woman."

Joe's face fell at her words. He stammered, "Oh...I see. Well, I guess I must've been reading things all wrong here. I thought that you and I... that there was a real connection."

Again, Maria interrupted Joe, not wanting him to get the wrong idea. "No, you read everything just right, Joe. I am so strongly attracted to you; I can't even find the words to properly describe it. Just let me explain fully, okay?"

Joe nodded silently for her to continue. "Like I said, technically I am still married on paper. But I've been in the process of getting divorced for a while now. That's actually why I was in Miami when everything happened - I was meeting with my attorney to complete the settlement details. This whole marriage has been over for years in my heart. I just never imagined I could meet someone like you and start having such strong feelings so quickly."

Maria placed her hand on Joe's arm reassuringly.

"I want you to know the full truth," she continued. "My husband and I grew further and further apart over the last few years. I finally filed for divorce after I found out he'd been cheating on me repeatedly. He became a different man from the man I married. It's like I don't even recognize him anymore. Honestly, I felt like such a failure. Like I must not have been giving him what he needed. The one thing I did know for certain was that I couldn't stay in that toxic relationship any longer. So, I filed for divorce. But he fought me every step of the way during the process. Frankly, at this point I don't even consider myself married anymore. My heart is free, even if legally I'm still tied to him."

She looked into Joe's eyes sincerely. "I needed you to know everything, Joe. Because I do have incredibly strong feelings for you that I can't ignore."

Joe had a solemn look on his face as he absorbed everything Maria had told him. "Ah, well I had a feeling this was all too good to be true. That's usually how things tend to go in my life."

He sighed deeply before continuing. "Let me be completely honest with you too, Maria. I have also been having some incredibly strong feelings toward you. It's like I'm under some kind of spell whenever I'm around you. When we touch, I just want to grab you, hold you close and kiss you."

Joe shook his head in frustration. "But I've held myself back because, well, I guess I was terrified that you didn't feel the same way. I just never dreamed..."

Maria grasped his hand tightly. "Joe, I do feel the same way, believe me. Please don't hold anything back from me. I promise to always be honest with you too. I'll tell you plainly right now - I've never been more certain of anything in my entire life. We are meant to be together, you and me. I know that probably sounds crazy since we barely know each other. But it's my truest feeling, straight from my heart. I know I'm already in lo-"

Joe squeezed her hand to stop her from completing the sentence. "Maria, please, don't say anything you might end up regretting later. Think carefully before you say something you can't take back."

Maria gave a little laugh. "Oh Joe, I've thought this through, believe me. I can't help how I feel. The truth is, I've completely fallen in love with you."

Joe looked into her dark eyes intently. "I never imagined I could find this kind of love again at my age. But I thank God every day for bringing you into my life. You've given me so much happiness and joy already. And yes, Maria, I love you too. I love you with all my heart."

Joe took a deep breath and continued. "Now in the spirit of full transparency, I should tell you that technically I too am still married in the eyes of the law."

Joe went on to explain how his ex-wife Paulette had left him and the kids when they were still quite young. She'd run off with her new boyfriend at the time.

"To get a divorce back then, we would've had to go through counseling sessions together, plus parenting classes - all sorts of hoops I didn't have time for as a single dad with two kids.

Paulette made it clear she didn't want custody anyway, so I didn't push the issue. I think she just wanted to save face with her family, make it seem like I was the evil ex holding the kid's hostage. So, I just let her spin whatever story she wanted. My only priority was taking care of my children, and I had custody at that point. Everyone seemed satisfied with the situation, so I just left it at that."

He shook his head as he continued. "I know the kids are grown now and I really should just file the paperwork and make it official after all these years. But honestly, I've just been putting it off, procrastinating. It wasn't exactly high on my priority list."

Maria had a look of concern on her face. "Is it because you still have feelings for Paulette? Do you still love her?"

Joe let out a loud, sarcastic laugh. "Ha! Good Lord, no. She put me through the wringer with her cheating. I forgave her so many times, but eventually I'd just had enough. The first couple of years after she left, I was filled with rage and bitterness toward her. But at some point, I realized I didn't hate her anymore. I was just...indifferent. That's the opposite of love, you know. Not hate, but apathy.

I don't wish Paulette harm, but I don't really care one way or the other about her life now. It sounds cold, and I'd never say it in front of the kids, but frankly I don't care if I ever see her again. We're strangers living separate lives. I'm completely indifferent to my ex-wife."

Maria nodded thoughtfully as Joe explained himself. When he finished, she gave him a little smile. "Well, it sounds just like earlier today, we were both in the same boat then and we're in the same boat relationship-wise now.

She squeezed his hand warmly. Joe pulled her close and kissed her tenderly. As their lips parted, he whispered, "I don't know where we're going, and I don't care, but I wouldn't want to be on this journey with anyone but you."

CHAPTER TWENTY NINE
TAKING ONE FOR THE TEAM

T he late afternoon sun beat down on Taylor as she walked briskly down the deserted highway, her eyes fixed intently on the distant horizon. Jake's words from earlier still rang in her ears: "We're so close babe. Looking at the map I think we can make it to the cabin by nightfall." After so much time, and so much hardship and uncertainty, the promise of finally reaching their destination filled Taylor with newfound hope and purpose.

Flanked on either side by Jake and little Parker, with Claire trailing quietly behind, Taylor felt electrified by the prospect of being reunited with her family again soon, especially her father. She and Joe had their differences over the years, that was for sure. He could be cynical, sarcastic, and often seemed convinced of society's impending doom. Yet through it all, she never doubted his love and commitment to protecting his family at all costs.

When the first rumbles of global catastrophe had started, Joe was the only one who seemed prepared. While Taylor chose to dismiss his worries at first, now she saw the wisdom in her father's ways. As the world descended into chaos around them, he had secured this haven out in the wilderness years prior. A safehouse for weathering the storm as he'd called it. How right he had been.

Lost in thought, Taylor suddenly turned to Jake walking beside her. "So, it's really only fifteen miles you think?" she asked, seeking reassurance.

Jake glanced down at the worn map in his hands, tracing their route with his finger. "That's right babe, no more than fifteen by my guess. We'll be kicking back with your pops by nightfall at this rate."

Taylor nodded, heartbeat quickening at the prospect. "Let's get moving then. I can't wait to see my daddy. He was so right about everything," she said, a renewed sense of urgency in her voice.

The foursome marched on as the sun sank lower on the horizon. An air of anticipation hung over them as they drew ever closer to the sanctuary Joe had prepared. Taylor could almost picture her father's grin of satisfaction, barely containing an "I told you so" upon their arrival. The thought made

Taylor chuckle to herself as she walked.

Claire had been uncharacteristically quiet most of the day, speaking only when necessary and keeping an alert watch over their surroundings. Taylor made an effort to fall back beside her at one point as they walked. "It won't be much farther now. Just hold out a little longer," she said encouragingly. Claire managed a thin smile and nodded, but her gaze remained distant, her mind elsewhere.

Taylor clapped her shoulder and let her be. She knew Claire was likely turning over that day's events in her mind, just as they all were. The confrontation on the highway that morning could have easily turned tragic if not for Claire. As they had been walking down the highway, they noticed a group of heavily armed drifters ahead, before they could scatter to the shelter of the woods, the group of men saw them. Claire said, "Wait here guys, I'll try to talk to them." Before they could protest Claire started walking ahead towards the men. As Taylor, Jake and Parker waited behind, Claire approached the men on the road. After a few minutes of talking to the men, Claire disappeared into the woods on the side of the road with what appeared to be the group's leader. Taylor and Jake, not knowing what to do, were terrified, they waited anxiously. After what seemed to be an eternity, the two emerged from the woods. Claire was visibly somber, walking with her head down. The group's leader signaled the other men to let them pass. Taylor and Jake had a pretty good idea of what had just happened as they started walking past the group of men. There was silence among them all as they continued their journey. Both Taylor and Jake were filled with all kinds of emotions, disgust, anger, sadness, disbelief but also relief and gratitude. Claire, they suspected, had done the unthinkable. They were mortified, yet so grateful for saving them all. Claire had literally put her body on the line to save them and their little girl from what could have been a very dangerous situation.

"Claire?" Taylor asked softly, "Do you want to talk about it?" Claire, with her eyes glistening with tears said, "Maybe someday Taylor, but not right now. I just did what I had to do."

Taylor with a reassuring arm around Claire said, "I understand, but remember two things, we are both here for you, when and if you do need to talk."

"Thanks Taylor, I appreciate that." Claire leaning her head on Taylors shoulder. "What's the other thing?"

Taylor stopped walking and turned to look

into Claire's eyes and said, "The other thing is you should know that Jake and I are so grateful to you for what you did today, for us, for Parker. Know that we will never forget that, and we are indebted to you forever."

Claire, looking back at Taylor with an appreciative smile said, "Thanks again Taylor, I've grown to really love you guys, and that sweet little kiddo of yours. Also remember I'm indebted to you folks as well, after all you saved me first, from basically the same fate, maybe it was just meant to happen, I'm just glad if it had to happen at least it wasn't for nothing."

As the sun slowly vanished below the horizon, the companions finally spotted their destination in the distance. Nestled among the trees atop a small rise sat the cabin. Taylor's heart leapt at the sight. This was it, their refuge. Their journey here had been perilous, but Joe's preparations had made their survival possible.

They reached the compound just as dusk settled over the wilderness. Claire took up a defensive position, scouting the perimeter while Jake and Taylor investigated the buildings ahead. The main cabin was even more impressive up close, solidly constructed from hand-hewn logs. An array of solar panels sat nearby, complementing the windmill generator atop a steel tower that rose above the trees. A true off-grid survivor's paradise.

Yet as wondrous as it all was, Taylor felt her elation dampen slightly upon finding the cabin empty inside. None of her family had yet arrived then. Were they even still out there? Would she see them again? The questions threatened to overwhelm her for a moment until little Parker toddled up and grabbed her leg excitedly. Taylor scooped up her daughter and held her close. They had made it here, that was enough for now.

Claire soon joined them, having confirmed the area was secure for the night. They barricaded the doors just to be safe before gathering in the great room. A warm fire now blazed in the massive stone fireplace as they ate a small meal from their dwindling provisions.

Though exhausted, Taylor's mind continued to race. She sat staring into the flickering firelight, Parker sleeping soundly on a pile of blankets nearby. Where was the rest of her family? Were Dad, Jojo and her grandmother safe? Would they all be reunited here like her father planned? She longed to see them so badly, yet the uncertainty of it all weighed on her.

Jake sat down beside her, and she leaned into him gratefully, taking comfort in his sturdy presence. He said nothing, simply wrapping an arm around her shoulders reassuringly as they watched the fire in silence. For all they had endured to get here, tonight it was enough just to be safe, and to hope.

CHAPTER THIRTY
KINDRED SPIRITS

P aulette and Alicia hurried along the cracked
asphalt road, eager to put distance between
themselves and the nightmare they had just
escaped at the gas station.

Alicia was still shaking, tears welling up in
her eyes each time the horrific memories flashed
through her mind.

"I'm so sorry, Paulette. I never should have run
up to that building without thinking," Alicia said,
her voice quivering. "It was so stupid of me. I put us
both in terrible danger back there."

Paulette reached over and squeezed the young
girl's shoulder reassuringly. "It's alright, dear.
What's done is done. We were lucky to have made
it out of there."

Paulette was still rattled herself, but she tried
to stay calm for Alicia's sake. That man had been
intent on doing more unspeakable things to them. It

was only by the grace of God they had managed to break free and escape while he was distracted.

"We have to be more careful from now on," Paulette continued. "It's not like it was. The world has changed. There are bad people out there who will take advantage of any vulnerability."

Alicia wiped the tears from her eyes, sniffling. "You're right. I won't run off like that again, I promise." She paused, looking hesitantly at Paulette. "Do you really think we'll make it to your ex-husband's place safely and what about your ex, they have a much longer distance to travel?"

"Of course, we will," Paulette said firmly. "And while my ex might have his faults, he's also one of the most stubborn and resourceful men I've ever known. If anyone can make it through a crisis like this, it's gonna be Joe Kelly."

Paulette thought back on her marriage to Joe. Regret still weighed heavily on her mind. Joe had always been so deeply devoted to protecting his family.

"There's nothing in this world more important to Joe than keeping his loved ones safe," Paulette laughed and said. "I know we had our problems, but I think deep down part of him still cares for me. At least enough to take us in when we arrive on his doorstep. I hope so anyway. " She said laughing.

Alicia looked at Paulette with concern. "You hope?"

Paulette smiled, "Don't you worry a bit, even if he throws me out on my ass, there's no way he could resist your adorable smile sweetie. He would not turn you out to be on your own, he's too protective a man for that."

"Paulette, if you go, I will go with you." Alicia said sternly.

Paulette with a big smile said, "You have nothing to worry about on that front, I'm sure Joe wouldn't even throw me out, deep down he's really nothing but a big softy."

Alicia managed a small smile. "You're amazing, Paulette. You were just ra - ra, after what you just went through, you can still laugh and stay positive." She brushed a few lingering tears from her lashes. "I hope one day I can be as strong as you."

Paulette waved her hand. "Oh, pish posh, it is what it is. You just accept what comes your way and keep putting one foot in front of the other."

She gave Alicia an appraising look. "But you want to know something? I think you've got more natural strength in you than you realize. With what you've already survived, you've proven you're a fighter."

Paulette put her arm around the girl's slender shoulders. "To make it in this new world, you're going to have to be even tougher than me. But something tells me you're going to do just fine."

Alicia blinked back more tears, but this time of gratitude rather than fear. She stepped forward impulsively and embraced Paulette.

"Thank you," she whispered. "I'm so glad I found you."

Paulette squeezed Alicia tightly. "And I'm glad I found you too, sweetie."

The two women stood hugging on the abandoned roadside for a long moment, drawing courage from each other. Despite the horrors they had endured since the pulse, they knew they could rely on one another. They had become like a mother and daughter, united in their determination to survive.

Finally, Paulette and Alicia separated. With a new sense of purpose, they continued walking steadily down the highway.

Step by step they progressed, focused only on moving closer to the sanctuary they hoped to find at Joe's remote cabin. They still felt lingering unease after what had just happened at the gas station, but together they found the strength to keep putting one foot in front of the other.

CHAPTER THIRTY ONE
BACK ON THE ROAD

The dawn's early light crept over the horizon, bathing the campground in a soft glow. Joe blinked awake, grunting as his back protested the hard ground beneath his sleeping bag. Though getting older had its downsides, today he felt younger than he had in years. The memories of last night with Maria played through his mind, bringing a smile to his weathered face. For the first time in too long, his heart stirred with possibility.

Joe sat up slowly, trying to shake off the morning stiffness. His lower back ached, but it was a small price to pay for the joy last night had brought. After two decades alone, the simple act of holding Maria in his arms felt like coming home. He had almost forgotten the feeling.

As he crawled out of the tent, Jojo was already up and moving, the army having instilled in him the habit of rising at the crack of dawn. Joe watched his son load their supplies onto the motorcycles with practiced efficiency, tightening straps and checking compartments. Pride swelled in his chest. Jojo had grown into a fine young man, strong and steady. Joe knew his ex-wife Paulette would be pleased too, if she could see the man their son had become.

Nearby, Maria began to stir as well. She caught his gaze and gifted him with a drowsy smile that made his heart skip.

"Good morning," she said softly.

"Morning," Joe replied. "Sleep, okay?"

"Better than I have in ages." A blush pinked her cheeks. Joe grinned.

"I'll start some coffee," Jojo said. Joe nodded in thanks as his son headed for the campfire ring to prepare their last hot morning beverage before departing.

Joe eased himself to his feet with a grunt and shuffled over to help pack up. He and Maria had agreed to let Toni sleep as long as they could before hitting the road. His mother was getting more fragile every year, though her spirit remained strong. The comfortable cot had done her good. He peeked into her tent, smiling as the small lump in her sleeping bag gently rose and fell.

He ducked back out quietly, not wanting to

disturb her rest just yet. Together, he and Maria finished securing the last of their gear while Jojo brewed coffee over the crackling fire. Before long, the rich, invigorating aroma filled their noses, banishing the last cobwebs of sleep.

Joe accepted a steaming mug gratefully, the heat seeping into his stiff fingers. He sank down on one of the logs encircling the fire and took a cautious sip.

"Perfect," he pronounced. Maria agreed as she swallowed her first taste.

Jojo joined them, blowing gently on his own mug. For a few moments, they simply enjoyed the quiet camaraderie and the peace that came with this in-between time, not quite dawn but not quite day either.

Joe let his mind wander back to the conversation he and Maria had shared the previous night. After years of building an emotional wall around himself, it had felt both terrifying and freeing to let it crumble. He knew without a doubt that he cared deeply for this woman, more than he had thought possible after so many years alone. The realization was equal parts thrilling and unsettling. So much could still go wrong in this chaotic new world. He tamped down the worries. All they could do was take this one day at a time.

While Jojo finished packing everything up, he glanced over to his dad sitting with Maria and could not help but smile. His dad deserved to find some love in his life. He had basically, been alone ever since mom ran off with that other guy. It was painful for sure for both himself and his sister Taylor, but dad also suffered from it as well. Sure, he had dated off and on over the years, but he was never able to find that one truly special person in his life and had quietly suffered with loneliness. Jojo hoped and prayed that this time everything would finally work out for his father. Maria seems to be smitten with him as well, so my fingers are crossed for them both. Dad deserves some love in his life.

After a time, Joe sighed and stood, back creaking. "Best wake your gram," he said. "Day's a wasting."

Jojo nodded and headed for Toni's tent. Joe turned to offer Maria a hand-up. She smiled softly and placed her hand in his. Her touch sent a pleasant tingle through his skin. He marveled again at how this remarkable woman could return joy to his heart so unexpectedly late in life. He couldn't guess how their relationship would unfold, but he was ready to find out.

They finished packing up the bikes as Jojo emerged with a sleepy Toni leaning heavily on his arm. Joe's heart clenched. She seemed to have shrunk overnight, her once sturdy frame now frail and unsteady. But her eyes glinted sharply as always.

"About time you slowpokes got moving," she teased. "These old bones can't take all this lollygagging."

They shared a laugh. Leave it to his cranky, tough-as-nails mother to be raring to go after the briefest of rests. The coffee and packing had energized Joe too, dispelling the last lingering fatigue. He straddled his Harley, reveling in the growl of the engine shuddering to life. Maria jumped on behind him, wrapping her arms tightly around his waist. Jojo and Toni climbed onto the second bike, his son taking the handlebars while his mother settled in behind him, clinging to his waist.

Toni produced a grin as she settled in. She gave her grandson a playful whack on the arm as she got situated. "Let's get this show on the road!"

Chuckling, Joe got under way. With a roar, their small caravan pulled onto the crumbling highway. For the first hour they rode at a steady but cautious pace, alert for any signs of danger, But the road remained empty, only the occasional small critter darting through the underbrush.

The further they went with no confrontation, the more Joe allowed himself to relax and enjoy the ride. Cruising these desolate roads reminded him of late-night travels in his youth, filled with a sense of freedom and adventure. With Maria embracing him from behind and his family close, Joe decided this battered new world wasn't so bad after all.

Around mid-morning, they reached a fork in the road. One way led northeast while the other cut a more direct line north towards their ultimate destination. Joe idled at the crossroad, peering down each weed-choked lane as he contemplated. Making a decision, he turned right toward the northeast fork. The way was rougher going but had more wooded cover, and after what they had already been through, he preferred the safety of staying off major thoroughfares, even if it cost them some time.

Joe smiled to himself as the bike leaned into the first curve. The dusty road took them deeper into a shady forest, the sunlight dappling through the canopy overhead. They hadn't passed a functioning fuel station in too many miles to count now, but the hog's tank was still nearly half full. Plenty to get them a good distance further. Maria's arms around him and his family close-by filled Joe with contentment. For the first time in forever, the future felt bright with hope.

An hour later, Joe's sharp ears detected a new sound rising above the rumbling engines and Toni's off-key singing - the unmistakable babble of running water. He raised a hand, signaling the others to slow. Soon they came upon the remains of an old stone bridge traversing a wide but shallow stream.

Joe pulled to a stop and killed the engine. "Let's take a break here," he said. The babbling water looked clean and pure, perfect for refilling their water bottles. Jojo had begun unstrapping their water containers as the others dismounted and stretched travel-weary muscles.

Maria was the first to spot it - a faded wooden sign nailed to a tree that read 'Myer's Creek'. She traced the carved letters thoughtfully. "Doesn't this creek seem familiar to you?" she asked Joe.

He scanned the tree line, memories stirring. "I think you're right," he said after a moment. "There used to be a nice little general store and gas station maybe half a mile up this road. Wonder if it's still standing?"

Jojo perked up. "We are getting low on supplies. Maybe we could check it out?"

Joe considered, then nodded. It was smart to restock when they had the opportunity. "Alright, we'll do it, but we proceed with caution in case anyone is squatting there. And we don't linger."

The others nodded. Joe helped Toni to her feet while Jojo and Maria splashed cool water on their sweaty faces and refilled the water. Refreshed, they remounted, and Joe led them slowly up the crumbling road, senses alert for any sign of inhabitants.

Rounding a bend, the remnants of the general store appeared. The gas pumps out front tilted at crazy angles, rusting with disuse. But the main building seemed largely intact, its weathered clapboard walls still sturdy beneath the sagging roof. Joe killed the engine again, listening intently. No sounds indicated people within.

"I think it's abandoned," he said quietly. "But stay sharp."

They approached cautiously, hands hovering near their holstered sidearms. The front door hung partially off its hinges, creaking faintly as it swayed in the breeze. Joe nudged it wider with his boot. Dust swirled in the angled sunlight piercing the gloom within. Shelves sagged under years of neglect, their scant remaining wares faded and cobwebbed. Toward the rear, a door hung ajar leading into what probably had once been the office. But nothing moved inside except drifting shadows.

Satisfied it was unoccupied, Joe beckoned the others to follow. Jojo immediately began inspecting the shelves and scavenging for any intact items he could throw into his pack. Maria peered behind the old front counter, coming up with a triumphant "Aha!" as she produced a large first aid kit. Toni shuffled down the aisles, plucking cobwebs from her wild white hair.

"Good find," Joe praised. His eyes scanned the interior, alert for hidden dangers, one hand resting casually near his holstered Colt. Though the place seemed picked over long ago, they were able to gather some useful items - a box of ammunition that matched Joe's .45, some faded but intact road maps, a forgotten bag of jerky, a lucky unopened bottle of aspirin.

Maria had slipped into the back office and gave a delighted cry as she appeared clutching two precious quart-sized containers of oil for the bikes. Joe's grin matched hers - that find alone made this detour worthwhile.

In less than twenty minutes, they had collected all that remained of value and secured it to the motorcycles. Joe did one last sweep, peering out through the dusty windows for any unwelcome observers. The road remained deserted.

"Let's move on," he declared. The others nodded, mounting up and glad to put the ghostly ruin behind them. Shortly the bikes coughed back to rumbling life, and they turned north again.

CHAPTER THIRTY TWO
A WELCOME RESPITE

Paulette and Alicia continued down the deserted highway, the sun beating down on them. Neither had eaten in over a day and their water bottles were nearly empty. Paulette could see the exhaustion in Alicia's young eyes. She knew they both needed to rest soon.

Up ahead, Paulette spotted a bridge crossing over a creek. "Let's stop up there and refill our bottles," she said, pointing toward the bridge.

Alicia nodded, too tired for words. They trudged on, finally reaching the cool shade beneath the bridge. Kneeling by the creek's edge, they refilled their bottles with the crisp, clear water.

"That hits the spot," Alicia said after guzzling nearly half her bottle in one go.

Paulette smiled, but it faded as she studied the girl. Alicia's slender arms were covered in scrapes and bruises from their harrowing journey so far. Her tangled dark hair hung limply about her smudged face. This was no life for a sixteen-year-old.

"We need to find you some food," Paulette said. "Get your strength back up."

Alicia gave a wan smile. "That would be amazing. I'm so hungry I could eat just about anything right now."

Paulette's heart went out to her. In the short time since they'd met, squatting on the side of the road with her head buried and broken in her arms, she'd come to think of Alicia as the daughter she had abandoned so many years ago. She had spent time with her kids over the years but not nearly enough. Her own selfish desires had blinded her as to what was really important.

"Well, we'll just have to keep our eyes peeled for anything edible as we go," she said, hoping to lift Alicia's spirits.

"Maybe we could try hunting?" Alicia suggested half-heartedly.

Paulette shook her head with a snort. "Neither of us would know how to go about that. Or have a weapon for it even if we did."

Alicia sighed. "You're right. I was just dreaming I guess."

Seeing her downcast face, Paulette tried to think

of a solution. Her gaze landed on the bubbling creek. That gave her an idea.

"You know, there could be fish in this creek," she said.

Alicia looked puzzled. "Fish? How would we catch them?"

"Back when Joe and I were first married, we used to go fishing all the time," Paulette explained. "I know the basics of how to do it. If we could rig up some makeshift poles, I bet we could catch us some dinner."

Alicia's eyes lit up. "Do you really think so?"

"It's worth a try. Some grilled fish would give us energy to keep moving. What do you say?"

Alicia nodded eagerly. "I say let's do it! But, um, how will we cook anything we catch?"

"No problem there," Paulette said, pulling a lighter from her pocket. "We'll build a small fire. I've started hundreds of fires over the years, Joe and I used to camp a lot and I was always the best fire starter for sure."

Alicia laughed. "Look at you, our wilderness survival expert!"

Paulette chuckled. "Well, I don't know about expert, but I know enough, I think." She paused; eyebrow quirked. "And anyway, if you get hungry enough, I hear raw fish makes great sushi."

They shared a laugh, the mood lifted. Paulette was glad to see Alicia's smile return.

"Better start gathering materials for those fishing poles then," Alicia said with a grin.

They got to work searching the area, looking for suitable branches and anything that could substitute for string and hooks. They broke off a couple of thin branches from the trees and then used their shoestrings to make a suitable fishing line.

Paulette said, "Now the hard part, what can we use for hooks?"

Alicia suddenly with a stroke of genius said "What about these pins, they were in my purse, and I just dumped them into my bag when I hit the road. We could bend them into hooks."

Paulette said, "Genius sweetie, that'll do nicely, perfect in fact."

Paulette started bending a couple of pins into the crude shape of a hook and said "We'll need one more thing sweetie."

Alicia, confused, said, "What."

Paulette said, "We're gonna need some kind of bait, something live and natural would be best if we can find something. Look around for any kind of bugs or worms or anything like that."

Alicia said, "That sounds totally gross, but I'm so hungry, I'll do it."

Within a few minutes the two had found a caterpillar, dug for a couple of worms and had even managed to find a beetle.

Paulette broke one of the worms into two pieces, baited her hook and did the same for Alicia saying, "Here we go, keep your fingers crossed."

"Now comes the real test," Alicia said. "Can we actually catch something with these homemade contraptions?"

"Won't know till we try." Paulette handed her one of the poles.

They found a clear spot along the bank and cast their lines out into the creek, watching their lines as they floated in the stream. Paulette felt a familiar thrill - it reminded her of many happy hours spent fishing with Joe and the kids back when their relationship was new and exciting.

After twenty minutes with no bites, Alicia was growing skeptical. "Are you sure there are fish in here?"

"Patience. We'll get something soon, I'm sure of it," Paulette said. Though secretly, she was starting to have doubts too.

Finally, Paulette felt a tug on her line. "Got one!"

she cried. She pulled the line in carefully, managing to pull a decent-sized bream from the water.

"Wow, it worked!" Alicia beamed at the flopping fish.

Paulette quickly removed the hook and handed the fish to Alicia. "Here, you gather some firewood. I'll keep trying for another."

Soon they had a fire going on the creek bank. Paulette speared the three breams they had caught on sticks and held them over the flames. The smell of the cooking fish made their mouths water. It had been so long since either had enjoyed a hot meal.

When the fish were nicely charred, they pulled them from the fire. Peeling off the blackened skin, the flesh underneath was moist and flaky.

Alicia took her first bite and closed her eyes in bliss. "Oh my god. This is so good," she murmured through a mouthful.

Paulette devoured her fish with equal relish. She watched the color return to Alicia's face as she ate. Paulette's heart swelled knowing she'd been able to provide this for her.

As they finished their meal, the sun dipped low on the horizon. Paulette yawned, suddenly overcome by exhaustion. Catching those fish had taken the last of her energy.

"Let's camp here tonight," Alicia suggested, reading her fatigue. "That was quite the feast. I think I can make it another day now."

Paulette nodded agreement, too tired to speak. They cleaned up their makeshift campsite as dusk fell. Then they hunkered down together under the bridge, sheltered beneath its concrete span. Tomorrow they would continue their journey. But tonight, bellies full, they slept more soundly than they had in ages. And Paulette dreamed of her family that awaited them, hopefully just a few days more down the road.

CHAPTER THIRTY THREE
OMINOUS WARNINGS

The successful scavenging stop had lifted their spirits. Joe laughed at something Maria called over the wind as the trees swept past in a green blur. The renewed energy propelled them onward at a good clip.

Around midafternoon, Toni began fidgeting in her seat as hunger pains gnawed at her belly. Joe took the cue and began scanning the sides of the road for somewhere to pull over and break for lunch.

Just then, the tree line fell away, revealing a small riverside clearing dotted with picnic tables. Joe banked toward it, the gravelly shoulder crunching under his tires as he pulled to a stop beneath the shade of a sprawling oak.

"This'll do," he said. The gurgle of the passing river promised fresh drinking water. As Toni, Maria and Jojo dismounted and began unstrapping their supplies, Joe knelt by the riverbank to splash his sweaty face. The chilled water felt glorious.

Maria was soon by his side.

"God, what I wouldn't give to strip down and use this river as my own personal bathtub."

Joe, with a wry grin said, "Not a bad idea sweetie,

I'd be more than happy to stand guard and keep a watchful eye on you. No, maybe, I should even join you, that way I'd be closer, you know in case you ran into any trouble, besides you'd probably need someone to help wash your back."

Maria looked at Joe, "I'll bet you'd be more than happy to do that for me." She continued dripping her words with sarcasm, "It's so nice to know that you would make such a sacrifice for little Ol' me Joe."

Joe chuckled with his own sarcasm, "Well, what can I say, That's just the kind of sweet guy I am."

Maria looking into Joe's eyes, "While this isn't really the right time or place, I do love the thought of it, and when we do find the right time and place and I pray it's soon, I promise we'll take that bath together, I mean after all, you were certainly right about one thing."

Joe looking confused, "I was right about what?"

Maria with a coy smile, "I will need someone to wash my back."

Joe laughed and as he was wiping his beard on his sleeve, Toni's panicked shout jerked him upright.

"Joe, get over here!"

He bolted for their cluster of picnic tables; gun already drawn as his eyes scanned for the threat. As he barreled around a tree, he found Toni pointing upward, face twisted in disgust. As the others arrived, they as well wore similar looks of revulsion. Joe followed their gaze up toward the oak branches, gun lowering as he spotted the source of their distress.

A man, or what remained of him, hung limply from a rope tied to a stout branch, swaying gently in the breeze. The body was in advanced stages of decay, writhing with maggots. The reek of death permeated the air even dozens of yards away. Fighting back bile, Joe counted at least six more putrefying corpses dangling nearby, all equally grotesque.

"Sweet Jesus," he choked out through the hand clasped over his nose and mouth. A makeshift graveyard, but for who? Criminals? Trespassers? Joe's mind spun with questions, but he had no intention of sticking around here to find answers.

Taking Toni gently by the shoulders, he turned her away from the grisly sight. "Come on, let's eat over here," he said gruffly, guiding her around the tree near the bikes. Maria still looked shaken as she helped unpack their lunch, hands trembling. Joe placed a steadying hand on her shoulder until the color returned to her cheeks. He doubted any of them would enjoy this meal after that gruesome find, but they had to keep their strength up.

"Not the scenic spot I had hoped for," Joe muttered, taking a seat on the picnic table bench. "But we'll just focus on chow."

The food's taste turned to ash in his mouth, but he forced himself to chew and swallow. At least the gentle babbling of the passing river gradually began to mask the imagined reek of decay that had permeated his nostrils. As soon as they reasonably could, Joe urged them to pack up.

"We're losing daylight. Let's put some miles behind us."

The others complied with visible relief, avoiding the hanging tree's line of sight as they finished securing their gear. Joe knew they were all still shaken, himself included. He decided finding a secluded spot to make camp for the night was their best bet.

Kickstarting his bike to growling life, Joe once again took the lead as their caravan pulled back onto the broken highway. The clearing's gruesome discovery haunted him as the miles passed beneath their wheels. What desperation could drive people to such acts? Or what cruel justice? He shook his head. Nothing good ever came from vigilantism. He only hoped whoever had strung up those poor souls was nowhere near. Distance was their friend.

By late afternoon, a worrisome engine knock developed in Jojo's motorcycle. At the next opportunity, Joe signaled to pull over. Lifting the seat, he frowned at the low oil level indicated on the dipstick. Though they'd topped it up fully just a couple days ago, the rattletrap bike was clearly burning through it faster than expected.

"Not good," Joe muttered, wiping the dipstick on a rag. "Must have an oil leak somewhere. She's near bone dry."

Jojo's face tightened with worry. "What should we do? We're still days from the cabin at least."

Joe chewed his lip, considering options. With nightfall approaching, time was short. "Tell you what - let's find a place nearby to hole up for the night. Come daylight, I'll take a better look and see if I can patch her up enough for us to limp home."

Jojo nodded, looking only slightly relieved. Joe clapped his son on the shoulder.

"Don't worry, we'll sort her out."

Another mile brought them to a narrow driveway leading off into a wooded lot. A weathered 'For Sale' sign lay canted in the weeds near the entrance. Joe guided his bike up the drive, finding a small clearing not far off the main road. The remains of a tumbled down cottage sat at the back, but the small field was otherwise clear.

"This'll work for tonight," Joe declared. Nearby, a branch of the river bubbled past, providing water.

As the others dismounted, Joe did a quick sweep of the ruined cottage and surrounding woods. Finding no recent signs of occupation, he waved the all-clear. The setting sun filtered through the pines, washing the sheltered clearing in a serene amber glow. They could not have found a safer spot to spend the night.

With Joe keeping watch, the others quickly set up camp. Maria got a fire crackling merrily, its warmth and cheery light raising everyone's spirits after the grisly events of the afternoon. Joe smiled as Jojo shyly offered to help Maria make dinner. Toni entertained them with off-color jokes, her laughter easing the lingering tension.

By the time they had eaten and tidied up, weariness had fully settled into Joe's bones. He was grateful they had time to properly inspect Jojo's ailing motorcycle. With Maria's help, he got Toni settled comfortably for the night then bid the others goodnight as well.

Crawling into his own sleeping bag, Joe felt the

day's exertions catch up with him. But rest did not find him easy. Each time he neared slumber, jarring images invaded - grinning skulls swaying from ropes, the soulless stare of the dead. Finally, he gave up trying to sleep. Rising, he added more wood to the glowing embers, staving off the night's chill.

The firelight cast flickering shadows onto the surrounding trees, igniting restless ghosts in their depths. Joe stared into the hypnotic flames, willing away the darkness in his own mind through force of will.

A hand on his shoulder made him start. Turning, he found Maria wrapped in a blanket looking at him with gentle concern.

"Couldn't sleep either?" she asked.

Joe shook his head ruefully. "Every time I close my eyes..."

He trailed off, but she understood. Settling beside him on the log, Maria slid her arm through his and leaned her head on his shoulder. Her solid warmth eased the chill in his bones. They sat that way in easy silence as the fire gradually burned down to glowing coals. Finally, Joe felt the tension in his shoulders begin to unknot. With Maria by his side, the ghosts retreated back into memory's shadows. No words were needed. Her simple presence was comforting enough.

CHAPTER THIRTY FOUR
JOJO'S PAST RETURNS

The morning sun streamed in through the dusty cabin windows as Taylor held two-year-old Parker in her arms, rocking the toddler back and forth. Though Parker seemed content enough, Taylor was worried. The long journey here from St. Augustine had depleted most of their food supplies. Now, in the light of day, the barren cupboards and near-empty pantry made it clear they needed to find more sustenance, and fast.

Claire and Jake looked equally hungry, having missed breakfast after waking up late. Taylor cleared her throat.

"We need to search every nook and cranny of this place," she declared. "I know my father, and Dad was always paranoid and over-prepared. He must have stockpiled supplies here somewhere."

Claire and Jake nodded in agreement.

"I don't even know your dad, but I've been

getting a pretty good idea of just how he operates, and I totally agree with you Taylor." Claire said.

Methodically, the three adults began scouring the cabin, opening up cupboards and rifling through closets in search of any hidden storage spaces Joe Kelly might have created. Little Parker watched the activity with curiosity, her big brown eyes following the adults' movements.

After twenty minutes of fruitless searching, Claire made a discovery in the back pantry. Grunting with effort, she shifted the shelving unit aside to reveal a trapdoor built into the floorboards.

"Jackpot," she said. "This must lead to a cellar or basement. Your dad wasn't messing around."

Jake stepped forward and tested the latch. The hinges creaked in protest as he forced open the stuck wooden door, revealing a ladder that descended into darkness below.

"I'll go first and check it out," he offered, pulling a flashlight from his pack. The women waited anxiously as Jake climbed down into the unknown space, the beam from his flashlight bobbing erratically over the walls. A minute later, his voice echoed up from below.

"Holy crap! This place is loaded with supplies."

Taylor exhaled, relieved that her hunch had paid

off. At her feet, Parker clapped excitedly as if aware of the discovery.

When Jake emerged, he described what he had found: rows of shelves lined with canned goods, bags of rice, boxes of ammo. All the essentials they needed to survive. Joe Kelly had not left his family unprepared after all.

Working quickly, Claire, Taylor and Jake formed a bucket brigade to haul some of the critical supplies up from the cellar. Cans of beans, vegetables, soup and more filled the kitchen counters.

"How long do you think this will last us?" Taylor wondered, taking inventory.

Claire did some quick calculations. "Rationed carefully, we could make these provisions last at least two or maybe three years if it's just us. A bit shorter if the others show up."

Taylor corrected Claire, "When the others show up!"

Claire sheepishly replied, "Of course, when the others show up."

With their most urgent needs now addressed, a sense of relief and hope filled the cabin. Even little Parker seemed to comprehend the importance of their discovery, helping stack cans like blocks while the adults planned the storage and rationing of the precious food.

Inspecting the ammunition boxes, Claire ensured they were also well-armed should any trouble arise. She spent the afternoon cleaning the array of firearms and making sure they were all in working order. No one would be catching them off-guard.

After enjoying a hearty meal courtesy of the newly uncovered stockpile, the group's morale lifted substantially. Full stomachs and the reassurance of ample supplies made their situation seem far less dire.

"I'm so thankful you two are here with me," Taylor said as they sat around the fireplace, watching the flames dance. "I don't know what I'd do alone trying to protect Parker."

"We'll get through this together, don't worry," Jake said, squeezing his wife's hand. Claire nodded in agreement.

Before turning in that night, Jake and Claire took precautions to conceal the trapdoor and camouflage the cellar entrance. If intruders ever breached the cabin, the hidden stockpile might be their saving grace.

With their bellies full, the small group slept more soundly than they had since the EMP knocked out power across Florida, plunging their lives into chaos. For one night, they felt almost secure.

The next morning, Taylor decided they needed to fully survey the cabin and surrounding area to take stock of what other resources might be useful for their survival.

Claire volunteered to scout the perimeter and check for any structural issues, sources of fresh water, or opportunities for trapping game. She headed out after breakfast, rifle slung over her shoulder.

The front door had barely closed behind Claire when Jake detected movement outside. Through the window, he spotted a lone figure appearing from the tree line some distance away. From the size and gait, it appeared to be a woman.

"Taylor, look," Jake said in a low voice. Taylor joined him at the window, squinting toward the distant figure. As she drew closer, they recognized the long blonde curls of none other than Jojo's ex-girlfriend, Abby.

"What the hell is she doing here?" Taylor hissed. The last time they'd crossed paths, Abby had caused no shortage of drama vying for Jojo's affection. Her presence now could only spell trouble.

Jake cautiously opened the front door with his gun at the ready as Abby approached with her hands raised. Though clearly exhausted, she offered a faint smile.

"Fancy meeting you two here," she croaked. "Any chance I could come in for some water? It's been a hell of a journey."

Taylor reluctantly allowed Abby inside, grilling her about how she came to be at their remote cabin and what she wanted.

Abby claimed she'd become homeless after the power went out and remembered Jojo's cabin and thought maybe she could come here and help. With limited options, she took a chance that Jojo would take her in.

Taylor informed her, "Well Jojo is not here, and frankly as his sister I feel the need to protect him from his own raging hormones, and you are definitely not what he needs right now."

"I'm sure you don't want me here, but I've got no one else," Abby said quietly, staring at the floor. She seemed sincere. Taylor begrudgingly agreed she could stay one night to replenish and move on.

When Claire returned from her perimeter check a short time later, she was introduced to Abby. Taylor then pulled Claire aside and filled her in on Abby and Jojo's past relationship. "She's nothing but a taker, she used her sex appeal to wrap my brother around her finger and then left when she found a better sugar daddy, she's a friggin' tramp and I want her out of here as soon as possible. I just feel so guilty throwing her out into the wilderness but damn her!"

Claire tries to calm Taylor, "Look it's none of my business and I don't know either your brother or this bimbo, but I have come to know you, and I know you'll be riddled with guilt if you throw this girl out on her butt. Maybe give her a chance, the world has changed, maybe she's seen the light."

Taylor reluctantly agrees, "Yeah I know, you're right, I'll try to control myself and give her a chance, but she damn well better pull her weight around here or she's out on her sweet little ass."

Taylor returned to Abby sitting at the kitchen table enjoying some food. "Listen Abby, I know you have a past with my brother and I'm praying that he'll be here soon. I also know that you dumped him for a better deal, I'm highly skeptical of you, but I'll allow you to stay, FOR NOW! But you better pull your weight around here and when Jojo gets back, he can decide what to do with you. Although I'm sure you'll manipulate him like you did before and he'll be eating out of the palms of your hands again just like before."

Abby, overcome with joy and wrapping her arms around Taylor's neck says, "Thank you so much Taylor, you'll see, I'm a changed woman. I regret losing Jojo and I'll do anything to win him back. You'll see, I promise I love your brother so much."

Over the next several days, an uneasy truce held between the women despite lingering tension. Abby made herself useful gathering firewood and helping mind Parker while Taylor prepared meals.

At night, Claire lay awake running through battle plans and contingency strategies should things go sideways. She had stockpiled an impressive array of weapons and Claymore mines from Joe's numerous stashes around the property.

Her vigilance soon paid off. Claire awoke near dawn to the urgent sounds of snarling and scuffling outside. Grabbing her rifle, she rushed out to see Abby single-handedly fending off a pack of three feral dogs with nothing but a hatchet.

Claire quickly dispatched two of the vicious creatures with clean shots. Abby swung her hatchet, sending the third limping back into the woods, howling in pain.

Adrenaline still pumping, the two women stood staring at each other, breathless.

"Thanks for the assist," Abby said sheepishly.

"Guess I let my guard down."

Claire gave a curt nod, then turned back toward the cabin without a word. After a moment, Abby followed too.

Nights were spent barricaded inside the cabin while Claire and Jake took turns keeping watch. By day, they foraged for edible plants, chopped firewood, and set snares for small game.

Taylor busied herself with caring for little Parker, keeping the cabin tidy and preparing whatever humble meals she could.

Abby pitched in somewhat, with watching Parker and helping in the kitchen with Taylor, but mostly she spent her time laying outside in the sun, in a skimpy bikini she had cleverly crafted from some bits and pieces of rags she had found in one of the linen closets.

After a few days of hunting, Jake was finally able to shoot a good-sized deer. The deer would provide them with precious meat.

After field dressing the carcass, Jake and Claire hauled the buck back to the cabin. Claire was an expert butcher, making quick work of skinning and processing the animal. Soon, venison was drying into jerky and strips of meat smoked over the firepit.

The smoky smell of cooked venison filled

the cabin, making their mouths water. At last, it seemed their fortunes were turning around. With sustenance from Jake's successful hunt, their food supply would now stretch a little longer.

That night, the group celebrated with a feast. Grilled venison, canned beans, rice and peas had never tasted so good. Laughter and cheer filled the cabin as they enjoyed the simple pleasure of a proper hot meal.

In the corner, little Parker gnawed happily on a piece of tender venison almost too big for her tiny hands. Taylor smiled, grateful to see color return to her daughter's cheeks. Each day their community grew stronger.

The venison surplus also allowed them to create a clever decoy for potential thieves. Jake had the idea to leave scraps of meat hanging outside the cabin when they were away. If anyone came across it, perhaps they would take the bait rather than investigating further for the real stockpile inside.

With stomachs full and their shelter now reasonably secured, conversation often turned to speculating what had become of the others.

Were Joe, Jojo and Toni still alive out there? Would they manage to complete the long journey from Miami?

Claire tried to reassure Taylor that if anyone could survive this catastrophe, it was her resilient family.

"Taylor, seeing what your dad has put together here, there is absolutely no doubt in my mind he will get his family here. I've never met him, but I feel like I know the man just seeing what he's done here."

Privately though, doubts gnawed at Taylor. She wondered how long they could manage to live off the land before their luck ran out. Would help ever come? Or were they now truly on their own in this strange new world? Was her family that she loved so much dead or alive?

The answers eluded them. But their only choice was to carry on, confronting each new day with determination to endure whatever obstacles came next. Together, they would find a way.

CHAPTER THIRTY FIVE
TROUBLE AHEAD

The morning sun peeked over the horizon, casting a warm glow over the makeshift campsite.

Joe slowly opened his eyes, becoming aware of a weight pressed against his side. Maria was nestled close, her head resting on his chest as she continued to sleep. The dying embers of their campfire smoldered nearby, tendrils of smoke rising lazily into the air.

Joe studied Maria's face, peaceful in slumber, a few wisps of dark hair falling across her cheek. His heart swelled looking at her. Even with all they had endured, just having her near made him feel like they could survive anything. Gently, he reached to brush the stray strands back from her face.

At his touch, Maria's eyes fluttered open. Meeting his gaze, her lips turned up in a soft smile.

"Good morning," she murmured.

"Morning," Joe replied, his voice still gravelly with sleep. "Sleep, okay?"

Maria nodded, then glanced around, taking in their surroundings. The road stretched on ahead, empty and desolate. Spotting Jojo and Toni still asleep nearby, she carefully sat up.

"I slept like a baby, I just can't believe we're so close to your cabin," she said. "Just one more day if we're lucky." "That's right," Joe confirmed as he too rose to a seated position. He winced slightly, joints protesting his night on the hard ground. "We'll be there soon enough. Just gotta get through today."

Maria placed a hand on his arm. "We will," she said firmly. "We've made it this far together."

Joe covered her hand with his own, gratitude welling up inside him. With Maria by his side, he truly believed they would make it.

Nearby, Toni began to stir, mumbling incoherently. Jojo remained motionless; his sleeping form leaned against a tree trunk.

"Suppose I better go check on the bike, make sure we're road ready," Joe said. With effort, he pushed himself to his feet, then extended a hand to help Maria up.

Jojo's motorcycle rested on its kickstand nearby.

Joe circled it slowly, inspecting every inch. The repairs he'd made last night seemed to be holding. Satisfied, he unscrewed the cap on the engine and checked the oil level. Still looking decent.

Rummaging through their packs, Joe found the bottle of motor oil Maria had scavenged from the abandoned gas station. Carefully, he added a bit more. He wanted to make sure they didn't run dry out here.

Replacing the cap, Joe did a final check. It wasn't ideal, but it would get them where they needed to go.

By now, Toni had woken and struggled to her feet. Maria was at the older woman's side immediately, offering an arm for support.

"Well, we're all up and at 'em," Joe called to the group. "Let's get moving as soon as we can."

Everyone worked quickly to break camp, eager to set out. As Joe kicked dirt over the smoldering fire, Jojo finally roused. Bleary-eyed, the younger man joined them.

"How's it looking?" Jojo asked Joe, nodding toward the bike.

"Good to go," Joe confirmed. "Made it through the night just fine. We're in business."

Jojo looked relieved. "Let's hit the road then."

The group gathered their packs and belongings. Joe did a final sweep to ensure they left no trace behind. Then Jojo straddled the motorcycle, kicking the engine to life. It roared satisfyingly.

Toni climbed up behind Jojo, holding onto his waist for stability. Joe and Maria mounted up as well.

"Alright, nice and easy," Joe called over as they pulled back onto the cracked asphalt. Jojo gave a thumbs up in reply.

They slowly continued their journey cautious and alert, senses primed for any sign of danger. The landscape passed in a monotonous blur - weedy roadside, fallow fields, abandoned farms. Joe kept an eye on the fuel gauge as it continued dropping. They needed to reach the cabin before it went dry.

Maria scanned the passing terrain anxiously.

They continued on. The morning hours slipped past uneventfully. Around midday, Joe estimated they must be getting close, barring any further catastrophes.

Just then, he spotted a barricade stretching across the road ahead. Cursing under his breath, he hit the brakes, throwing up a hand to signal Jojo. They rolled to a stop, idling roughly fifty yards back.

"Dammit" Joe growled. He exchanged an uneasy

look with Maria.

Jojo had gone stock still atop the motorcycle, poised for action. After a beat, a handful of armed men appeared from behind the blockade, weapons raised menacingly.

CHAPTER THIRTY SIX
BROTHERS IN ARMS

Jojo rolled his motorcycle up next to his father's, with Toni perched on the back. They slowed to a stop and studied the situation ahead warily. A makeshift barricade of junked cars, old furniture and other debris blocked the two-lane road, manned by six armed men who stood resolute, rifles in hand.

"I don't see any way around them," Joe said grimly.

Jojo nodded. "They aren't advancing or seeming too aggressive towards us. It's very strange."

From behind, Maria suggested nervously, "Maybe we should just turn back and try to find another route."

Joe shook his head. "That'll add hours to our trip, with no guarantee the next road won't be blocked either."

Jojo pondered for a moment before saying, "Dad, I've got an idea. Gram, get off the bike. I'm gonna ride up there solo and feel them out. You all stay back here for now. At the first hint of trouble, you get the ladies out of here fast."

Joe's brow furrowed with concern. "I don't like it son, it's too dangerous."

"I've been trained for situations like this, remember?" Jojo said. "Don't worry, if I get a bad vibe, I'll hightail it outta there quicker than you can spit. Then, we'll have to find another way."

Joe sighed; his eyes troubled. "I really don't like this plan, but I understand your thinking. Proceed with extreme caution. Maybe, God willing, we can talk our way through this peacefully."

Jojo edged the motorcycle slowly forward, one hand hovering over the holstered pistol on his hip. He stopped about fifteen yards from the barricade and called out, "Hello there!"

A gruff-looking man with a bushy beard stepped forward. "Hello to you too, stranger. What can we do for you folks today?" His tone was more relaxed than Jojo expected.

"Well, to be honest, we'd love to pass on through without any unpleasantness," Jojo said evenly. "We're just trying to get back home, a bit further north of here."

The bearded man shook his head. "I'm afraid that's too dangerous. This area's gone to hell."

Before Jojo could respond, the man's words were suddenly drowned out by a shout from behind the barricade.

"Bones! Bones, is that you?"

Jojo tensed, his head swiveling towards the source of the voice. Bones was an old army nickname he hadn't heard in ages.

A tall, lean figure appeared from the tree line beyond the barricade, waving an arm excitedly. As he drew nearer, Jojo broke into a shocked grin, at once recognizing the man's face. It was his Army buddy Sam, a fellow Florida boy he'd bonded with during their deployment but lost touch with over the years.

Jojo kicked the bike back into gear and rode to meet Sam, hopping off to exchange a fierce bear hug with his long-lost friend. Their delighted laughter rang out as they clapped each other on the back. With a wave to the others, Jojo signaled that it was safe to proceed.

Joe, Maria and Toni slowly and cautiously made their way forward. They gathered around the barricade, casting wary glances at the ragtag band of locals who eyed them silently, firearms at the ready.

Sam gripped Jojo by the shoulders, beaming ear to ear. "Well, I'll be damned, Bones! Never thought I'd run into you again, especially not out here. How the heck have you been?"

"Hangin' in there, trying to keep my family safe, same as everybody," Jojo said. "Hell of a surprise running into you too. What's your story?"

Sam nodded grimly. "I was visiting my uncle's place a few counties over when everything went to shit. Been hunkered down with these folks ever since, trying to keep our little community safe."

He turned to the leader of the group. "Earl, you can stand down. These here are friendly folks."

Earl lowered his rifle and the rest of the men followed suit. "You vouch for them, they're vouched for. We can't be too careful these days." The rest of the group relaxed marginally as Earl cracked a faint smile. "Nice to see some new friendly faces around. Name's Earl. This here's my boy Chet, my brother Paul, our friends Odie, Lincoln and Felix."

The ragtag defenders nodded in greeting. Jojo made quick introductions of his own family and companions. An air of wary relief settled around the group.

Sam stepped closer, lowering his voice. "You folks heading up north like you said? Because you do not want to continue on this road, believe me. The town up ahead has been completely overrun. Gangs of looters running wild, taking whatever, they want. Attacking anyone passing through."

Joe's jaw tightened. "I was afraid it might be something like that. We got turned around a ways back trying to avoid trouble. This seemed like our quickest and hopefully safest way north."

Sam nodded. "I understand, but luckily you stumbled on us first. Come on back to our camp, we can get you some food and supplies. Map out a safer route avoiding the hot zones."

Jojo clapped his buddy on the shoulder. "We'd appreciate that. Lead the way."

The motley defenders dismantled a section of the barricade to allow the vehicles through. Earl waved them into a small caravan. "Let's get you folks off the road. Ain't safe to linger out here in the open these days."

They followed the locals' trucks through the trees, arriving shortly at a small encampment dotted with tents and vehicles. Women and children peered out curiously at their arrival. Sam made more introductions as they were welcomed into the modest but cozy community.

Over a shared meal of smoked venison, canned goods and fresh bread, Sam and the locals described the deteriorating situation in the area. Food and supplies were running low. Desperate refugees and violent gangs were ever increasing. They recommended an alternate route well east of the overrun town, through sparsely populated backroads and forests.

"It'll take you out of your way, but you'll avoid the worst of it," Earl said, tracing his finger along the map.

Joe nodded gratefully. "We appreciate the advice. And your hospitality." He turned to Sam. "We can't thank you enough for stopping us back there. This changes everything."

Sam grinned. "Of course, Bones here is like a brother to me. Any friend of his is a friend of mine."

After a bit more discussion over the map, Jojo stepped away from the group with Sam. "Really lucky we stumbled across you all, don't know what we would've rolled into if you hadn't stopped us."

"Just glad I could return the favor after all you did for me overseas," Sam said quietly. He hesitated before continuing in a somber tone. "You saved my life more than once. I will never forget that."

Jojo shook his head dismissively. "We looked after each other, like soldiers do. I know you'd have done the same."

"Of course." Sam clasped his friend's shoulder. "Still, finding you again now, it feels like divine intervention. We'll make sure you all get where you're going safely as we can. After that..." His voice trailed off.

"After that, you should come with us," Jojo said suddenly. "I mean it brother, there's strength in numbers and we could use someone with your skills."

Sam looked thoughtful. "That's kind of you to offer. Let me sleep on it tonight. We can talk more before you head out."

"Deal." Jojo pulled him into another quick hug before they rejoined the others.

The group spent the night camping around a cozy fire, taking comfort in a newfound community. Sam promised to see them off safely at first light. As Jojo gazed around at his family and friends, his heart swelled with gratitude that they'd been brought together for this chance reunion when they needed it most. He said a silent prayer of thanks for the blessing of old friends and new allies in such troubled times. With Sam's help, they now had a real fighting chance of making it the rest of the way home.

CHAPTER THIRTY SEVEN
PLAYING WITH FIRE

The pale light of dawn filtered through the trees as the group began stirring in the early morning chill. Joe emerged from his tent, groaning softly as his joints cracked. At 59, sleeping on the hard ground wasn't getting any easier.

He saw that Sam had already had a fire going and was setting up pots of coffee and oatmeal. The rich, earthy smell made his stomach rumble.

"Mornin' Joe," Sam called out. "Coffee's just about ready."

"Bless you, son," Joe said, holding his hands out toward the flames. "Nothing better on a chilly morning."

The others gradually emerged from their tents, drawn by the promise of hot coffee. Maria came out still rubbing the sleep from her eyes. Toni hurried over, grabbed a cup of coffee and got bundled up in a blanket to keep warm.

Once they had all eaten, Jojo pulled Sam aside for a private talk. "What else can you tell me about those gangs that have taken over the town up ahead?" he asked.

Sam's expression darkened. "A nasty bunch, the lot of them. They call themselves the Scorpions and the Rattlers. They've turned the whole place into a war zone."

He went on to explain how the gangs terrorized the townspeople, forcing them into slave labor and stealing their food and supplies. The younger women also suffered unspeakable abuse.

"Do they ever work together or are they always at each other's throats?" Jojo asked.

"Oh, they hate each other alright," Sam said. "You couldn't get them to agree on the time of day. They've split the town right down the middle with the main street as the dividing line."

Jojo nodded thoughtfully. "So, if some incident provoked one side to cross into the other's territory, would they fight it out?"

"Hell yes, they'd tear each other apart," Sam said. "Had a couple of real bloody battles so far over petty squabbles."

A sly grin spread over Jojo's face. "I think I know how we can take those bastards out and free that town."

Sam looked puzzled for a moment before realization dawned on him. "Wait, you don't mean..."

"Oh, I surely do," Jojo said. "You boys happen to have any rifles with decent scopes?"

Sam laughed and slapped Jojo on the back. "Oh, you bet we do, and we've got some crack shots among some of these good Ol' boys too, I think we're gonna get along just fine. Come on, let's go talk to Joe."

The two men gathered everyone together to outline Jojo's bold but dangerous plan. He proposed using scoped rifles to pick off gang members and make it look like the rival side had perpetrated the killings. Done right, it would spark an all-out war between the Scorpions and the Rattlers.

"It's risky," Joe said, folding his arms over his chest. "Things could easily spiral out of control. Innocent folks could get caught in the crossfire."

"They already are," Jojo countered. "At least this way we'd be freeing them from these monsters once and for all."

"I don't know..." Maria said uneasily. "This seems like playing with fire. What if you just make things worse for the townspeople?"

Toni spoke up in support of the plan. "Jojo's

right. This might be their best chance to take back their town. I say we help them fight."

Back and forth the debate went on, with good points on both sides. In the end, the majority agreed that the plan, while extremely risky, could work. With the gangs gone, the people would have their town back.

"Alright, let's do this," Joe said finally. "But we've got to do it clean and smart. No collateral damage. Understood?"

Everyone nodded solemnly. Lives hung in the balance, but with courage and skill, they could pull this off.

Jojo grinned, ready for action. "Let's go bag ourselves some snakes."

The group spent the next hour hammering out planning. Sam knew the lay of the town well and directed them to an old clock tower that offered a clear vantage point over Main street. It stood just a block back from the dividing line between the two gangs' territories.

Earl, Chet, and Paul would provide cover while hidden inside an abandoned storefront window, while Jojo, Sam, and two of the other men climbed the tower with rifles. Toni and Maria would stay back out of harm's way with the rest of the group.

Joe took up a rooftop position with Lincoln and Felix halfway down the block to scout and relay information by walkie-talkie.

When all were in position, Jojo peered through his scope at the street below. He could see members of both gangs loitering on their respective sides. This would have to be executed perfectly.

"Alright, here we go," he murmured. "Let's start a war."

Jojo and the marksmen carefully pick off members of each gang, making it appear the rival side is responsible. Tensions ignite quickly and a fierce battle erupts between the Scorpions and Rattlers as intended.

Joe helps coordinate from his rooftop perch while Earl, Chet, and Paul provide cover fire from their position in the storefront when needed. They narrowly avoid collateral damage by warning innocent townspeople to take cover inside buildings.

After a bloody clash that leaves many gang members dead or wounded, the survivors retreat, realizing they've been duped.

With the gangs severely weakened, the townspeople emerge from hiding and flood the streets and start taking back control of their town.

Jojo and Sam watched from high above in the

clock tower beaming with pride.

They watched as men chased and at times brutally executed several of the wounded gang members.

The dangerous gamble had paid off.

CHAPTER THIRTY EIGHT
RECRUITING SAM

The sun beat down on Main Street, where a feeling of relief and jubilation hung in the air. The battle was over, and the town was safe, at least for now. Joe, Jojo, Sam, Maria, Toni and the rest of the weary but triumphant townspeople congregated in the center of town, slapping each other on the back and letting out shouts of excitement.

Adrenaline still pumping through his veins, Sam suddenly yelled out, "Wolverines!"

Jojo shook his head and chuckled. "Really, a Red Dawn reference?"

Sam laughed loudly. "What the hell, it seemed appropriate."

"Yeah, you may be right," Jojo conceded with a grin. His army buddy's enthusiasm was contagious.

As the celebration continued around them, Jojo led Sam aside to speak privately. "Sam, is there anything holding you here? Why don't you come with us? We're heading to my father's cabin. It's remote, defendable, fully stocked and hopefully safe."

Sam's smile faded. He hesitated, shifting his weight as he considered the offer. "Wow, I really appreciate that Bones, but I feel like I'd be intruding. I mean it's your family place and all."

"Sam, you are family and besides, we can use another well-trained military guy for sure. You'd be an asset, not a liability. Please come with us," Jojo implored, placing a firm hand on his friend's shoulder.

After a pause, Sam finally nodded. "Ok, I'd love to join you guys, but you have to run it by your pops first."

Right on cue, Joe walked over to the pair. Though he hadn't meant to eavesdrop, he'd overheard the tail end of their conversation. "Not that I was eavesdropping, but you are very welcome to join us, Sam. Like Jojo said, you'd be a great asset to our group, and what the hell, you seem like a pretty good guy. So, is it settled?"

"Absolutely, sir," Sam replied with a respectful nod.

Jojo had to stifle a laugh at his ramrod straight

posture.

Joe waved his hand dismissively. "Joe, just call me Joe."

"Yes sir," Sam responded automatically.

Shaking his head in amusement, Joe turned and walked away. The young man's earnest politeness reminded him so much of Jojo when he'd first enlisted. Some things never changed.

The celebration lasted long into the night. As the adrenaline finally wore off, exhaustion set in for Joe and the others.

When the first hints of daylight peeked over the horizon, Joe called everyone together. It was time to start the long journey to the cabin.

After heartfelt goodbyes with the people of Dundee, Joe, Jojo, Sam, Maria and Toni piled into a battered but trusty old van they'd claimed from the town's garage. Although the van had no keys, Jojo was able to get it started by hot wiring the ignition.

Joe asked with a look of concern, "Son I hate to ask this, and maybe I don't want to know, but where did you learn to hotwire cars?"

"You're right Dad. You don't want to know. Jojo said grinning from ear to ear. "Let's just say it's the product of a misspent youth and leave it at that."

Joe stood still looking a bit stunned and said,

"Well it certainly paid off for us today, I guess. But someday son, I'm gonna want to hear that story, but for now, Let's roll."

Joe took the driver's seat with Maria beside him navigating. Jojo and Sam rode in the middle seats while Toni stretched out on the far back seat.

The van rattled and bounced over the pitted backroads, weaving around abandoned cars and debris. Joe kept one wary eye on the rearview mirror, on high alert for threats. Conversation was minimal, the mood apprehensive.

About ten minutes into the drive, Maria looked down at the map and then out at a passing road sign. "Joe, we can continue on US twenty-seven, and it is a bit more direct, but also a lot more populated. Looking at the map, I think if we took state road thirty-three, while it does add a few more miles it looks much more remote, and I don't really think it will take that much more time in the long run. What do you think?"

"I think whatever route you feel is the best way to go, I'm with you, you have my complete trust." Joe said, smiling.

Maria said, "Are you flattering me again, sir?"

Joe said, "Absolutely, but it is also true, I trust you completely."

Maria replied, "Then keep your eyes peeled for the turn off on the left side for state road thirty-three, it should be coming up in a few miles, and thank you."

Joe nodded, following her directions, and found the turn off a few minutes later. As the van slowly rolled onward, Jojo glanced back and saw Toni wince, her face pinched in pain. "You okay Gram?" he asked with concern.

"Oh, I'm fine dear, these old bones just don't like all this bumping around," Toni replied, trying to sound upbeat. But the deep creases in her face betrayed her discomfort.

"Dad, let's take a break and stretch our legs for a few minutes," Jojo suggested. Joe agreed, pulling the van off to the side of the road near a grove of trees.

Everyone gratefully climbed out and worked the kinks out of their muscles. Toni waved off offers of help, taking only Sam's arm for support as she hobbled around. After a short rest, they piled back into the van and continued on.

The further they drove from Dundee, the more desolate their surroundings became. Periodically, they passed through abandoned towns full of looted, burned-out buildings. Nature was already reclaiming the land, sprouting up through cracks in the pavement. It was an eerie sight.

Around midday, they stopped briefly to refuel the van from gas cans in the back. As Joe poured gas, Sam and Jojo kept vigilant watch for any hostiles. Thankfully, the area appeared deserted.

Back on the road, miles of rural forest rolled by outside their windows. The trees grew so dense it felt as if civilization was being swallowed up behind them.

"There's the turnoff for Route nineteen, just past that utility truck." Joe exhaled in relief at the sight of the upcoming landmark. They were making progress. The final stretch at last.

As the van passed the empty truck, Sam's muscles tensed. His sharp eyes caught on something - the glimpse of a face in the truck's side mirror, watching them.

"Ambush!" Sam yelled just as bullets pierced the van's back windows, shattering glass across the seats.

CHAPTER THIRTY NINE
TRIAL BY FIRE

A s Sam cried out and the bullets shattered the van's rear window, Joe stepped on the gas pedal hard, his foot pressing the aging accelerator down to the floorboard. The old engine roared in protest, but the rusted blue van lurched forward with a sudden burst of speed.

It was clear from Sam's shout and the tinkle of breaking glass that the gunshots had come from the muddy white utility truck they'd just passed on the lonely stretch of rural highway. Joe hazarded a quick glance in the rearview mirror, seeing the truck already pulling onto the cracked asphalt behind them, its hood ornament glinting cruelly in the harsh midday sun.

"Floor it, Dad!" Jojo yelled from the passenger seat, bracing one hand against the back of Maria's seat while he twisted to look out the back of the van. His face was creased with tension, hazel eyes narrowed as he kept his focus on the pursuing truck.

Joe didn't bother responding, his lined face set in rigid determination as he coaxed every possible ounce of speed out of the weary vehicle. The old van shuddered violently, the shocks groaning from the sudden increase in velocity. Outside, the cracked concrete highway blurred by in a streak of gray.

Still the utility truck accelerated aggressively, its powerful engine growling as it rapidly gained on them. For it, the frantic chase was as easy as stomping a bootheel on an ant. Within bare moments, the massive grill loomed large in the van's back window, close enough for Joe to see the rust stains and missing paint.

"He's gonna ram us!" Jojo snapped, half rising from his seat as he twisted to look out the back. One hand hovered near the hunting knife sheathed at his belt.

Joe's eyes flicked back to the mirror, watching the truck close the distance as easily as a shark chasing a wounded seal. The front bumper was mere feet from their back doors, the shattered glass clinging to the window frames the only barrier between them.

"Hang on!" Joe yelled, hands yanking the wheel sharply to the right as he pulled the van onto the gravel shoulder. Loose rocks spit and clattered as the tires left the pavement, fishtailing on the uneven surface. The utility truck shot by them, its horn blaring angrily at being denied its prey.

As the larger vehicle surged past, Sam popped up from behind the back seat, rifle braced on his shoulder. With the short hair and muscular build that betrayed his military background, his green eyes were hard and utterly calm as he smoothly tracked his target. The AR-15 cracked sharply three times, muzzle flashes leaving wisps of smoke.

The truck's back window exploded as two of Sam's shots punched through the glass and into the passenger side, sending crimson splashes across the truck cab's interior. The driver jerked the wheel reflexively, veering halfway into the opposite lane before overcorrecting just as quickly. The truck crossed the highway at an angle and barreled onto the opposite shoulder, kicking up a cloud of dust and loose gravel before plunging nose-first into a rocky ditch.

Sam ducked low in the back again, waiting tensely. A moment later, the crippled truck erupted in a sudden fireball, orange flames and greasy black smoke clawing at the sky as the gas tank detonated.

"Hell yeah, that's what I'm talkin' about!" Jojo whooped, pounding the seat like a kettle drum. He grinned over at Sam, eyes alight. "Nice shootin', Tex!"

Sam just gave a mild nod, his expression neutral as he clicked the safety back on his smoking rifle. "Just trying to pull my weight, sir," he said in his usual laconic drawl.

Despite the younger man's nonchalance, Joe knew Jojo's praise meant a lot to the former soldier. He met Sam's gaze in the rearview mirror, scarred features softening fractionally.

"We'd have been buzzard food without you, son," Joe said solemnly. "Much obliged for watching our six."

Pink tinged Sam's tanned cheeks at the unexpected thanks, but he simply nodded again, settling back down out of sight like the consummate soldier he was.

Joe guided the van back onto the pitted highway, hands steady on the wheel despite the lingering tremble of adrenaline in his veins. He blew out a slow breath, pulse pounding loud in his ears. After a few miles, he risked a wry half-grin over at his son. "Remind me not to piss that boy off."

Jojo laughed, some of the tension easing from his shoulders now that the immediate threat was past. He winced slightly as he dabbed at a few small cuts on his hands and arms from the flying glass shards.

Turning in her seat, Maria noticed blood covering Jojo's arm, she reached to gently take his wrist.

"Here, let me see, Jojo," she murmured, expertly plucking a sliver of glass from one of the scrapes with a pair of tweezers retrieved from the med kit at her feet.

Jojo flinched but held still as the petite woman tended to him, her dexterous hands working quickly and efficiently. Maria's dark ponytail slid over one shoulder as she leaned closer to apply antiseptic to the minor wounds, her brow faintly furrowed in concentration.

Despite Jojo's half-hearted protests that he was fine, Maria insisted on bandaging his larger cuts, shooting the younger man a stern, no-nonsense look when he tried to pull away. Jojo's cheeks flushed, but he submitted meekly to her ministrations after that, mumbling his thanks when she finally released his hand.

Maria smiled warmly in response before shifting her attention to checking on Toni. "How about you Toni, any injuries back there?"

"You don't have to worry about me dear, other than my heartbeat being through the roof right now, I'm fine." said Toni.

Up front, Joe kept his focus on the road unwinding ahead, hands locked on the wheel in a white-knuckled grip. The memory of the truck looming behind them in the mirror, ready to crush them off the road, replayed in his mind. He knew they'd barely slipped the noose this time, but thanks to Sam's combat instincts and steady aim, they had made it yet once again.

Yet they couldn't hide from the world forever. Joe knew getting his family to the secluded cabin was their only real chance of riding out the chaos spreading since the lights went out for good.

So, he forced his doubts and fears down deep, concentrating only on the miles left between them and refuge. Whatever dangers lurked ahead, he would do whatever it took to protect his loved ones and keep his family alive. For now, that meant focusing only on the cracked and weathered highway unfurling steadily beneath their wheels, drawing them closer to the sanctuary waiting ahead.

They were so close now. Joe blinked sweat from his eyes and kept on driving.

CHAPTER FORTY
SANCTUARY AT LAST

As the van bumped along the last few miles of dirt road leading to the cabin, Maria gazed out the window taking in the thick forest surrounding them. She turned to Joe in the driver's seat and said, "I think we're getting really close now."

Joe glanced down at the map spread across his lap, tracing their route with his finger. "You're right sweetie, we're very close," he replied. "I recognized those last few turns. We should be pulling up to the cabin in just a couple of miles."

Maria's eyes widened in surprise, and she let out a little laugh. "Did you just call me sweetie?"

Joe's face flushed red with embarrassment. "Uh, yeah sorry about that. I didn't mean to be out of line or too familiar."

"No, don't be sorry. I liked it," Maria said, placing her hand gently on Joe's arm. "It felt good to hear a kind word like that. It's been a while."

Joe looked over at Maria, her olive skin glowing in the sunlight streaming through the trees. His eyes lingered on her face, taking in every curve and detail. A warm admiration and longing to know this woman better stirred inside him.

"Well in that case, I'm glad sweetie," Joe said softly. "And you know what else is going to make you feel good?"

Maria's eyes widened again, and she exclaimed in a playfully scolding tone, "Joe!"

Joe let out a bellowing laugh. "No, no, not that! Though we'll certainly discuss those thoughts of yours a little later. I meant we're pulling onto my driveway right now. We've finally arrived at the cabin, just like I promised you we would."

Maria shook her head and laughed, her cheeks flushing a little pink herself. Joe grinned and called out excitedly to the others packed in behind them, "Hey everyone, we've made it! We're home!"

There were cheers and sighs of relief from Jojo, Sam and Toni. As the van crunched along the gravel drive, they all peered out at the impressive log cabin nestled amongst the tall pines. Smoke wisped up from the chimney signaling someone was inside. But, who?

CHAPTER FORTY ONE
REUNITED

The van rolled to a stop and the front door swung open. Taylor came bounding out with Parker toddling along behind her, their long hair blowing in the stiff breeze.

"Daddy, you made it!" Taylor exclaimed as she ran up to the van. Joe hopped down from the driver's seat and embraced his daughter tightly.

Right on Taylor's heels, little Parker shrieked "Gampa, Gampa!" Joe released Taylor from the hug and scooped Parker up, giving her a big kiss on the cheek.

"Grandpa made it just like he said he would. And he's so glad you and your momma listened to him for once and got here safe and sound," Joe said, hugging his granddaughter close.

Taylor gave her dad's shoulder an affectionate squeeze. "We're doing great now Dad. I can't tell you how relieved I am to see you."

By now Jojo had exited the van and come around to give his little sister a bear hug, nearly lifting the petite Taylor off her feet.

"Oof, easy there big brother! You're actually choking me," Taylor gasped dramatically.

Jojo set her down chuckling. "Ah come on sis, you know you love me."

Taylor smoothed her rumpled shirt and replied sarcastically, "Yes, Jojo, I'm absolutely thrilled to see your ugly mug." Then she cracked a smile and added more sincerely, "But honestly, I really am glad you're here safe." Tears began to flow from her eyes as the emotions of the moment started to overwhelm her.

Joe put his arm around his two grown kids, an enormous sense of relief washing over him at having his family together again. He did a quick round of introductions between Sam, Maria and the rest of the group already at the cabin.

Meanwhile, Jojo's attention was drawn to the attractive athletic blonde who had quietly come around the side of the cabin to get a look at the new arrivals.

"Well, hello there, who might you be?" Jojo said, giving Claire an appreciative up-and-down glance.

Taylor smacked her brother's shoulder playfully.

"Down boy. That's Claire. She had some trouble, and we took her in. She's been a huge help to us here and on our journey here as well."

Jojo rubbed his shoulder, still grinning. "Is that so? Well maybe Claire can give me a hand later too. I'd sure appreciate any help she wants to offer."

Taylor just shook her head knowingly. "I'm sure you would, Romeo."

Just then the cabin door creaked open again and out sauntered a curvaceous blonde wearing nothing but a skimpy bikini. Jojo did a double take as the woman called out in a singsong voice, "Jojo! You made it!"

It was none other than Jojo's impulsive, drama-prone ex, Abby. Jojo muttered under his breath, "Well shit."

Taylor gave her brother a wry smile and patted him on the back. "Have fun dealing with your hot mess of an ex, big bro. She's all yours."

Jojo scratched his head and sighed as Abby ran over and threw her arms around him. "Yeah, this ought to be interesting."

He disentangled himself from Abby's grasp and held her at arm's length. "Abby! What the hell are you doing here?"

"Looking for you, silly!" Abby exclaimed, trying

to nestle closer to Jojo again. "After everything went dark, I just knew I had to find you so we could face this thing together."

Jojo gently pushed Abby back again. "Abby, you and I haven't been together for over a year. I'm not sure why you'd think..."

Abby waved her hand dismissively. "Oh, who cares about ancient history. We have something special; you just haven't realized it yet."

Over Abby's shoulder, Jojo noticed Claire standing near the van watching this exchange unfold with a raised eyebrow. He felt his cheeks flush hot with embarrassment.

"Listen, Abby..." Jojo started but she grabbed his arm and began pulling him towards the cabin.

"Come on, I'll fix you a drink and we can catch up. I'm dying to hear about your heroic adventures getting here!"

Jojo hesitated, then relented and let Abby lead him inside. As the door swung closed, he shot an apologetic glance back at Claire. This was going to take some delicate handling to let Abby down easily without causing a scene.

Meanwhile, Joe supervised the unloading of all the supplies from the van into the cabin's large pantry. He was anxious to take stock of their food situation.

Toni sank down slowly into a rocking chair near the fireplace, grateful to rest her aching bones after the long uncomfortable ride. Maria brought her a blanket and helped prop up her swollen feet.

"There you go dear, just try to relax now that we're here safe and sound," Maria said softly.

"Bless you child," Toni said, patting Maria's hand. "I'll be right as rain after I get some food in my belly and a proper sleep in a real bed."

In the kitchen, Taylor and Jake were busy preparing a hearty venison stew from the deer they had shot earlier that week. The rich aroma filled the cabin, making everyone's mouth water. Little Parker sniffed the air then tugged insistently on her mom's pant leg.

"Mama, I'm hungwy!" Parker whined.

"I know baby girl, it's almost ready," Taylor said, scooping Parker up and giving her a slice of apple to tide her over. "Why don't you go play with your dolls by Great Grandma Toni for a few minutes?"

Parker wiggled down and scurried off, apple wedge clenched in her little fist. Taylor smiled watching her go, then returned to tending to the deer meat on the stove.

Jake added chopped potatoes and carrots to the bubbling pot of broth. "Looks like your brother has his hands full with Abby, huh? I think he'd rather be back out on the road," Jake jokingly said.

Taylor chuckled. "I think you could be right. But he's got a good heart under all that bravado. I'm sure he'll handle it well; well, I hope he'll handle it well. That girl loves to bring the drama."

Jake smiled and kissed Taylor on the cheek. "Well, if he takes after you, I'm sure he'll handle it like a pro."

Taylor laughed sarcastically. "If only! We're about as different as night and day. But blood is blood. And I really am glad he's here."

Jake gave the stew a final stir then said, "I think this is ready. Let's get everyone fed!"

After a hearty meal together, spirits were high around the fire as the group swapped stories about their journey. Bellies full and bodies exhausted from the day's events, it wasn't long before yawns started rippling around the room.

Joe stood up and stretched. "I think it's about time we all got some shut eye. We can figure out sleeping arrangements in the morning, but tonight let's just grab any open bed or sofa we can find."

Maria started unfolding the hide-a-bed sofa while Sam and Jojo grabbed some extra quilts and pillows from the linen closet.

Toni was already sound asleep and snoring loudly in the recliner. Jake carefully tucked a blanket around her.

Soon the cabin filled with the soft sounds of sleep - the crackling fire, Toni's muffled snores, and Jake's rhythmic breathing next to Taylor in bed. Claire slipped outside into the night to take the first watch, guarded but comforted by the feeling of finally having found a safe haven.

The next morning, pale gray light filtered through the windows as the group awoke slowly. Joe was up before the sun brewing a pot of coffee over the fire. The rich aroma roused Jojo from his spot on the floor. He sat up with a groan, rubbing his sore back.

"Rise and shine, sleepy head," Joe said, handing his son a steaming mug. "We've got a long day ahead getting this place secured."

One by one the rest of the group shuffled into the kitchen area, gratefully sipping mugs of hot coffee. Jake stood at the griddle frying up venison sausage and powdered eggs while Taylor sliced some bread to toast over the fire.

"Eat up everyone," Joe said, shoveling a heaping pile of eggs onto his plate. "We've got a lot of ground to cover today."

After breakfast, Joe gathered everyone around to lay out the plan for the day. "Jake, Jojo and Sam, I want you three checking the perimeter - make sure the fences are secure, no breaches anywhere. The cold weather will only get worse, so we need to button up any gaps."

The men nodded and headed out to do a lap around the extensive property. Joe continued, "Taylor and Maria, you two inventory the pantry and take stock of our food supplies. See what we have and where we're short."

The women got to work sorting through cans and boxes on the shelves. Joe turned to Claire. "We need more firewood split and stacked. There's a big deadfall about a quarter mile west in the forest. Take an ax and a cart and let's get a cord chopped and loaded."

Satisfied that everyone had their assignments, Joe got to work himself securing the shutters over the windows and checking the generator's fuel supply.

By mid-afternoon, chores were complete. The team gathered for a quick bite, weary but satisfied by the progress made. Jojo gave Claire a playful nudge and asked, "Say, you want to take a break and go for a walk? Stretch our legs a bit?"

Before she could answer, Abby swooped in and clutched Jojo's arm possessively. "What a fantastic idea! We'd love to go for a romantic stroll in the woods together." She shot Claire a smug smile.

Claire pursed her lips, then replied evenly, "You two go on ahead. I'm going to clean my rifle." She stood up and headed inside.

Jojo watched her go, shaking his head. He untangled himself from Abby's grip as she tried to pull him towards the trees.

"Abby, hold on. We need to talk about this."

Abby pouted dramatically. "Talk about what? I just want to be close to you again Jojo."

Jojo took a deep breath, choosing his words carefully. "Listen, I know you want to pick up where we left off, but you and I were over a long time ago. I've moved on and I think you need to also."

Abby's eyes filled with crocodile tears. "But Jojo, I came all this way for you! I risked my life for us to be together." Her voice rose louder, carrying through the woods.

Jojo shushed her gently. He could see Taylor, Maria and Sam exchange smirking glances over this juvenile drama unfolding.

"You didn't risk anything for me. You made your own choices. Now I'm making mine - we're not getting back together." Jojo said firmly.

Abby stomped her foot. "You can't mean that! Tell me you don't love me!" She lunged forward to kiss him.

Jojo quickly side-stepped her advance. "Abby stop! This isn't going to work. I'm sorry if that hurts you, but I've made up my mind."

Abby gasped dramatically, tears rolling down her cheeks. "You're a monster! I never want to speak to you again!" She turned and flounced off into the woods.

Jojo sighed, shaking his head. Dealing with Abby was exhausting, but at least she finally got the message. Now hopefully things could settle down around here.

After Abby's tantrum, an awkward silence hung over the group. Maria gave Jojo a sympathetic smile and squeezed his shoulder reassuringly.

"That couldn't have been easy. But you handled it with sensitivity and grace. It had to be done, I'm proud of you," she said.

Jojo smiled back gratefully. "Thanks Maria. Hopefully the drama is behind us now."

Just then a bloodcurdling scream rang out from the direction Abby had stormed off. Jojo's stomach dropped. Oh no, what now?

The group jumped up and sprinted towards the screams. They skidded to a halt in a small clearing where Abby was desperately fending off two men, their ragged clothes and deranged eyes marking them as marauders.

One man had Abby pinned while the other tried grabbing her flailing limbs. Jojo didn't hesitate. He lunged forward and tackled the second man to the ground. They grappled violently until Jojo smashed his head against a rock, knocking him unconscious.

Meanwhile Sam wrestled a knife from the other man's grip, allowing Abby to scramble free. Sam whipped the blade handle against the man's temple, and he crumbled to the ground.

Panting hard, Jojo hurried over to Abby. "Are you okay? Are you hurt?" He searched her face with concern.

Abby flung herself against Jojo's chest, wrapping her arms around him tightly. "You saved me! I knew you still loved me," she cried.

Jojo gently unfastened her grip on him. "Whoa, I was just trying to help. You'd have done the same for any one of us."

Abby gazed at him adoringly. "But it was you who saved me, my hero!"

Before Jojo could respond, Claire stepped

forward and took Abby firmly by the shoulders. "You've been through a trauma. Let's get you back to the cabin so you can calm down."

Claire shot Jojo a knowing look as she led Abby away. Jojo gave her a grateful nod, glad to have the buffer. Hopefully Abby would start to see reason once the shock wore off.

"Claire!" Jojo shouted as she walked back towards the cabin, "Could you send my dad down here with some rope when you get back, we need to figure out what to do with these two guys once they come to."

"Sure thing Jojo." Claire yelled back.

CHAPTER FORTY TWO
NEW LEESBURG?

As Jojo waited for his father, he started doing a quick search of the men as they lay unconscious. They had no weapons, but he did find that they each had several cards in their pockets.

"Jojo, Claire filled me in, I brought some rope." Joe said as he arrived by his son's side.

Joe holding up the cards he found in the men's pockets asked his father, "Dad, what do make of these?"

Joe took the cards and began to study them. "It looks like they are some kind of redemption coupons or something. Good for one meal, Good for one shot, Good for fifteen minutes with grade "C"."

"What the hell is grade "C"?" Jojo asked.

Joe spoke slowly, "I have no idea son, but they've got a handful of these with all kinds of various things listed. They are all signed the same way."

"They're signed?" Jojo asked

"Yeah", Joe responded, "At the bottom of each of these it's signed, Chuck Warner, Mayor of New Leesburg."

Jojo with a stunned look on his face said, "New Leesburg, what the hell is that, and who the hell is

243

Chuck Warner?"

Joe looked down at the two unconscious men and said, "I have no idea, but maybe these two can fill in some blanks when they come to. Sam, run up to the cabin and grab Jake to help us get these two secured in the shed for the night. Maybe we can get some answers in the morning."

CHAPTER FORTY THREE
GOOD COP BAD COP

Throughout the night, Joe, Jojo and Sam rotated keeping guard in front of the shed where they had bound and gagged the two attackers.

When morning broke, Joe and Jojo arrived back at the shed bringing a freshly brewed pot of coffee and mugs to share with Sam.

As they sipped the strong coffee, they began to map out their strategy to extract information from the two men they had apprehended the night before.

Joe blowing on his steaming coffee asked, "Ok guys, so how do we proceed, any ideas."

Sam piped up immediately, "Well sir, I've been thinking about just that thing the last few hours of my guard shift and it seems to me, we go with an old classic."

Jojo looks confused, "An old classic, what the hell is this old classic?"

Joe, swallowing a mouthful of coffee says, "I think what Sam is referring to is Good cop, bad cop, and please no need for the sirs Sam, just call me Joe."

"Yes sir, I will do that si uhm…Yes, Good Cop, Bad Cop is exactly what I was thinking sir."

Joe chuckled, "Well I guess you're making progress; I think. Ok, I like that idea, now let's figure out who's good and who's bad."

"Well sir, uhm Joe, I think I can pull off the bad cop role if it's all the same to you. I've been practicing for the last hour going over scenarios in my head. I think with a mix of bad and with a little crazy mixed in, I can scare the hell out of these guys."

"Sam, I agree, I think you can indeed pull that off, because I'm not so sure you'll be acting." Joe said laughingly.

"Thank you, sir." Sam said proudly.

Joe looked at Jojo and said, "I guess that makes you and I the good cops, kiddo."

Jojo nods in agreement and says, "I'm good to go, I'll follow your lead dad."

CHAPTER FORTY FOUR
EARLY MORNING INTERROGATION

Joe swung open the creaky wooden door of the shed, letting pale morning light stream onto the two disheveled men huddled against the far wall. Their hands were bound behind their backs and their ankles tied together with coarse rope. Both gagged with dirty rags. Blood and grime streaked their faces, and their clothes were torn and filthy.

The men squinted against the light as Joe stepped inside, followed closely by Jojo and Sam. Joe noticed the men stiffening at the sight of Sam - his imposing stature and the wild look in his eyes seemed to unnerve them. Good, Joe thought. Let them be on edge.

Joe cleared his throat and pulled the gags from each man's mouth. "Morning gentlemen. I hope you got some shut eye, cause you've got a long day ahead of you."

The men exchanged wary glances but remained

silent. Joe continued. "Here's the deal. You're gonna tell us everything you know about this New Leesburg situation, and who this Chuck Warner fella is who seems to be running the show over there."

Again, only silence from the men. Joe nodded to Sam, who cracked his knuckles menacingly.

"My friend here gets really antsy when folks don't cooperate. So, I suggest you start talking, unless you want him to help loosen your tongues."

The smaller of the two men spoke up timidly. "Please mister, we don't want no trouble. We'll tell you what you wanna know, just please keep him away from us." He eyed Sam fearfully.

Joe smiled. "That's more like it. Now first off, names."

The little man licked his dry, cracked lips. "I'm Mitch and that's my buddy Cal." Cal gave a curt nod but stayed quiet.

"Alright Mitch, tell me about this Chuck fella. How'd he end up running that town?" Joe asked.

Mitch shifted against his bindings. "Aw hell, Chuck's always been an operator. Even before all this, he had his hands in a bunch of businesses - some legit, some not so much. He knew how to wheel and deal."

Cal added gruffly, "He's real charmin' too.

Makes people wanna follow him, do what he says. When things first went to shit, he stepped right into that power vacuum."

"So, he saw an opportunity and seized it?" Joe asked.

"Yessir. Gathered up some rough customers, promised 'em rewards if they helped him take over. Once he had muscle on his side, weren't nobody left with the stones to stand up to him," Mitch said.

Joe felt anger simmering in his gut. The idea of this Chuck exploiting good folks turned his stomach. "And just what kind of rewards did he offer?" Joe asked, keeping his voice steady.

Mitch looked down at his lap. "Aw you know, stuff like extra food or liquor. Better living quarters away from the riff raff. And uh..." His voice trailed off.

"Go on," Joe said firmly.

Mitch's face flushed. "Also, women. The lookers, he keeps for his top guys. Let's 'em...have their way."

Joe clenched his fists, fighting to maintain control. Jojo muttered curses under his breath.

"It's true," Cal snarled. "We seen it with our own eyes. Chuck's got a whole stable of fillies he passes around as party favors. It's disgusting."

Mitch gave Cal a warning look but stayed silent. Joe contained his boiling anger. Now was not the time to lose it.

"What about the women who refuse these arrangements?" Joe asked through gritted teeth, though he feared he already knew the answer.

"Then it's forced. Chuck don't take no for an answer once he sets his sights on a new gal. Anyone who kicks up a fuss...they aren't around long"

Joe exhaled slowly, looking at the ground. When he raised his eyes again, they had hardened into cold steel.

"You seem real forthcoming with information all of a sudden," Joe said to Cal. "Why the change of heart?"

Cal held Joe's icy gaze unflinchingly. "Cause what I seen there turned my stomach. Beating on folks weaker than you, taking what ain't yours...that ain't me. I only rode with Mitch here on account of us going way back. But Chuck and his whole operation can go straight to hell."

Joe considered this, then gave a curt nod. Perhaps an alliance could be forged here after all.

"One more question before we move on. What's the story with those coupon cards you boys were carrying?" Joe asked.

Mitch piped up again eagerly, seeming relieved to shift the subject. "It's like a reward system Chuck dreamed up. The more work you do for him, the more coupons you earn. Then you can cash 'em in for stuff."

"Women included, I gather," Joe said darkly. Mitch nodded, not meeting his eyes.

"It's true. Based on what you do for Chuck, you get coupons for different lengths of time with the women. The women are branded from "A" all the way down to "F" like grades," Mitch confirmed.

Joe tilts his head and looks at Mitch, "You use the term branded?"

Mitch says, "Yes they are actually branded, with a tattoo A through F."

Jojo exploded. "You mean you brand these poor girls like cattle? Force them into prostitution?"

Jojo is enraged, "What a pig, can you imagine the humiliation of being branded and with an F no less. So, I imagine, with this coupon you get 15 minutes with a C graded woman? To do what?"

Mitch shrunk back at Jojo's outburst. ""Anything you want. They also have coupons for shorter and longer periods of time, the better you perform for the mayor, the more time or higher-grade women you can get, it's all at his discretion of course. We don't do the branding! That's all Chuck and his top men. We're small time, just take the scraps passed down to us."

Joe asked, "What brought you gentlemen here?"

Mitch said, "We saw that cute little blonde walking this way and we thought she would be a grade A girl for sure and maybe if we brought her back, we could gain some favor with the mayor."

Sam chimed in, "But she's been here a few days, what were you doing all that time?"

One of the men answered, "We've been here watching trying to figure out a way to get to her, when all of a sudden she walked right into our camp, we couldn't believe it."

"So, who else knows you're here?" Joe asked

"We came alone on a whim after spotting blondie walking this way."

Joe stood up. "Thank you, gentlemen." We'll get back to you, let us talk outside for a few minutes."

Cal said, "Mister, we're really sorry, we didn't mean any trouble. If you just let us go, we'll be on our way and you'll never see us again, I swear."

Joe looked at them solemnly, "Thank you for that, that's good to know."

Joe, Jojo and Sam step outside.

"Dad, what do you want to do with these two?"

Jojo asked.

Joe looked at Jojo and Sam with a grave face, "grab a couple of shovels and have them each dig a hole, then shoot them in the back of the head."

"Dad, are you sure?" Jojo asked incredulously.

Joe looked at Jojo sternly, "Do you want them coming back or bringing others back with them and trying to grab Abby or any other women we have here? Jojo, think about what these guys would do with your sister if they ever got a hold of her and let that thought help you pull the trigger. There is a New Leesburg, and this is a New World."

Sam said, "Understood sir."

CHAPTER FORTY FIVE
DIGGING THEIR OWN GRAVES

After grabbing two shovels, Joe, Jojo and Sam enter the shed. Joe says, "Get these vermin on their feet. We're going for a little walk."

Sam roughly hoisted Mitch and Cal up. Joe led the way outside into the brisk morning air. He nodded at Jojo, who tossed shovels at the men, "Start digging." Joe told the men.

When the graves were ready, Joe turned to face Mitch and Cal. His face was grave.

"You both seem like decent enough men caught up in an indecent situation," Joe began. Mitch looked hopeful, while Cal held his stoic expression.

"This New Leesburg you all have built on the backs of the weak - it ends today, I'm truly sorry for this but you both had a choice. You could do the right thing and fight against evil, or you could join the forces of evil. You both made your choice willingly;

you both chose the easy way. I can't gamble with my family's safety that you will make the right choice next time, given your previous choice and your obvious weaknesses" Joe continued.

Realization dawned on Mitch's face as Joe unholstered his revolver. He began whimpering pleas for mercy. Cal simply lowered his head silently. He had known this was coming.

Joe's arm remained steady. "Your friend Chuck and his whole operation have corrupted the very soul of Leesburg. The only justice left is at the end of my gun barrel. I'll see you both on the other side."

With that, two quick shots rang out. Mitch and Cal slumped lifeless to the ground. Sam hauled their limp bodies into the waiting graves and shoveled dirt overtop.

As the last bit of loose earth was patted down, Joe let out a long, shuddering breath. He had dispensed the only justice left in these dark times, but that didn't make it any easier to bear.

Joe turned to his son, placing a hand on his shoulder. "I'm sorry you had to witness that, son. But this is our reality now. We do what must be done to protect our own."

Jojo met his father's eyes. "You did right, Dad. It's like you said - this is a new world."

Joe pulled Jojo into a tight hug. Over his son's shoulder, Joe asked "You alright too, Sam?"

"10-4, sir. We're fighting the good fight," Sam replied somberly.

Joe gave Sam's back an appreciative pat as they headed back to the cabin. Though his heart was heavy, Joe walked with purpose. Hearing of the depravities happening in Leesburg only strengthened his resolve to fortify this haven they were building.

He would be ready when Chuck Warner's reign of terror inevitably turned its attention their way. And he would show the same mercy he had granted Mitch and Cal today. The time for talking was over. It was time to send a definitive message about what happens when you threaten his family and their community.

Joe only hoped the others would understand the justice he was duty-bound to enact. That it went against his very nature, but these were no longer normal times. He had to become as hard as the world Chuck Warner had created in order to save the light left.

As the cabin came back into view through the trees, Joe steeled himself. He would do whatever it took to protect this place and these people. And God help anyone who stood in his way.

CHAPTER FORTY SIX
PLANNING A PATH AHEAD

I nside the cozy cabin, the mood was light. Maria tended to breakfast on the wood stove while little Parker tottered about underfoot. Taylor sat prepping food at the table, laughing with Claire as Jake dramatically reenacted his confrontation with a curious raccoon the night before during his perimeter check.

Toni snored gently in her rocking chair by the fire, wrapped in a quilt. The hard lines on her face had relaxed into a soft peacefulness. Even Abby seemed in brighter spirits, humming to herself as she arranged some wildflowers in a vase on the mantle.

The lively chatter dimmed some when Joe entered with Jojo and Sam. His grave expression told them the interrogation had gone even worse than anticipated.

"Let's gather around. We've got some things to

discuss," Joe said wearily, pulling up a chair. He motioned for Sam and Jojo to sit as well.

The group quietly found seats; faces etched with concern. Joe blew out a long breath before beginning to recount all he had learned about the new mayor of New Leesburg's exploits.

Gasps and murmurs rippled around the room as Joe shared the details. The women hugged their arms around themselves protectively at the mention of the vile subjugation and branding of the town's women.

Jake and Sam clenched their fists, eyes burning with rage. As Joe described the coupon reward system, Claire leapt up, unable to contain her fury.

"That's it. We have to put an end to this monster and his whole sick regime, now!" she burst out.

Murmurs of agreement followed her outburst. Joe held up a hand. "Believe me, nothing would satisfy me more than seeing this guy get a long overdue helping of justice. But that's easier said than done."

"Why not form a militia?" Sam proposed. "With the manpower we have here, and the weapons and tactical training between Jake, Jojo and myself, we could-"

"Are you nuts?" Taylor interrupted. She gestured

emphatically around the room. "Half our group is children, elderly, injured! How could we possibly mount any kind of assault?"

Sam shook his head firmly. "This ain't the old world no more. They've shown their true colors. If we don't stamp this out now, they'll just prey on more innocent folks."

Lively debate erupted as the group passionately argued for and against taking direct action against the mayor and his cronies. Joe sat back, letting the debate unfold organically. These weren't decisions he could make unilaterally anymore.

Maria's soft voice cut through the chaos, commanding the room's attention. "Enough arguing. Nothing can be accomplished like this." She stood and faced the group.

"Sam is right - action is needed to stop a great injustice. But Taylor raises a fair point too. We must be strategic in how we respond."

Murmurs of assent followed her remarks. Maria continued, "Together we will find an appropriate solution. But it will take time, thought and courage from all of us."

Joe smiled inwardly with pride at Maria's wisdom and composure. She would make an exceptional leader for this community. He resolved at that moment to start grooming her for that role.

Maria moved to Joe's side, placing a gentle hand on his shoulder. "Why don't we take a breath and regroup over breakfast? We can't solve this on empty stomachs after the long night you all had."

Joe covered Maria's hand with his own gratefully. "You're absolutely right, as always. Let's reconvene after we eat."

The group disbursed, emotions still running high, but the edge taken off by Maria's calming presence. Joe approached Toni's rocking chair and gently woke her so she could join them for the meal.

"Rise and shine, Ma. Let's get some food in that belly," Joe said softly, helping Toni to her feet. She gave his hand an affectionate pat as they made their way slowly to the table.

Over a hearty breakfast of powdered eggs, instant mashed potatoes and venison sausage, the mood lightened as conversations turned to reminiscing about better times and hopes for the future. Laughter flowed freely again, filling up the empty spaces the darkness of this new world had seeped into.

Stomachs full and spirits lifted, Joe once more called everyone together. "Alright, let's talk this through with clear heads now. I want to hear from each of you."

He nodded to Sam first. "It's obvious that action must be taken. But we have to be smart. Get intel on their operation from the inside before we strike. Maybe even turn some of his disgruntled men against him."

When he finished, Joe gave the floor to Taylor. She stood, holding Parker on her hip. "I just keep picturing more mothers like me, terrified for their children if we kick this hornet's nest. We have to consider who will bear the brunt of retaliation."

Parker babbled in agreement, eliciting soft chuckles from the group. Joe then looked to Claire for her perspective. She hesitated, then spoke.

"This guy and his men are undoubtedly dangerous. But cornered rats bite hardest when threatened. We can't become like them in our quest to remove their threat." Murmurs followed as they digested her insight.

One by one, Joe asked for everyone's point of view. Jake advocated fortifying their position for the long haul. Toni surprisingly advocated a strong offensive attack before things got worse. Jojo and Abby both struggled with decisive opinions, seeing merit in arguments both for and against action.

Maria spoke last. "This affects us all. But the final

decision lies with you, Joe. We trust your judgment as to the best course of action."

All eyes turned to Joe. He stroked his beard thoughtfully before standing.

"You've all raised fair points. This is no easy choice," Joe began. "I vowed to always protect my family and our home. But open war brings suffering to both sides."

He paced slowly as all watched intently. "We need time to gather information, shore up our defenses here, and build alliances. Then, if negotiation fails, we'll be in a better position to act decisively."

Murmurs of agreement followed his remarks. Joe felt the weight of leadership heavy, but Maria and the others had validated his more measured approach.

"It's decided then. We prepare for trouble but try for peace. Together we'll get through whatever comes next," Joe said.

Resolute nods answered him. Joe's chest swelled with pride for this ragtag group that had become a family. They would face down this threat and any danger side by side, of that he was now certain.

Over the next few days, the community worked tirelessly to implement Joe's vision for preparation and defense.

Jake and Jojo reinforced the perimeter fencing and built a secondary inner gate. Toni, Maria, Taylor and Abby spent long hours starting a sizable garden using seeds Joe had stored in the hidden pantry below the kitchen. Sam and Joe took shifts scouting the surrounding area and training together to hone their tactical skills. Parker scampered around underfoot, taking special joy in "helping" Claire clean weapons and set hunting snares.

At night, they sat around the fire sharing stories, laughter and songs. A sense of hope filled the cabin, despite the looming threat. For the first time since everything fell apart, they felt in control of their collective destiny instead of just trying to survive day to day.

Joe made a point to pull Maria aside one evening after dinner. He needed to be near her. He had been so busy the past few days that he hadn't had time alone with her. They sat together on the porch swing gazing up at a sky full of brilliant stars.

"I want you to know how much I value your wisdom and level head, Maria," Joe said, taking her hand. "In times like these, communities need strong leaders they can believe in."

Maria nodded thoughtfully. "The people here, they believe in you, Joe."

"Yes, for now," Joe replied. "But someday they'll need someone new to guide them. Someone like you."

Maria squeezed Joe's hand but stayed silent, letting his words settle over her. She had never desired power or leadership, content to serve in her own humble way. But Joe was right - if called to it, she would step up and do what was needed.

Joe slipped his arm around her shoulder and pulled her close. Maria rested her head against him, cherishing the simple joy of this quiet moment together amidst so much uncertainty.

CHAPTER FORTY SEVEN
REFUGEES ON THE HORIZON

T he next day brought unexpected developments. Sam returned just before dusk from an extended reconnaissance mission, bringing urgent news.

"We've got visitors incoming," Sam announced. "I spotted a small group, maybe a dozen folks, making camp two miles to the north of us. They seem to be refugees fleeing Leesburg based on what I overheard."

Joe's eyebrows raised in surprise. "Refugees are welcome here, provided they intend no ill will. Sam, take Jake and scout their camp first thing tomorrow. Discreetly. We need more intel before making contact."

Sam nodded. "You got it. With any luck, we'll gain some allies out of this bunch. Lord knows we need all the help we can get with what's coming."

That night, Joe lay awake long after Maria

had drifted off beside him. Sam's report troubled him. These refugees might bring valuable inside knowledge of Chuck Warner's operation. Or they could be a Trojan horse sent to infiltrate their compound. It was a precarious line to walk.

Joe eventually slipped into a fitful sleep, his mind churning endlessly through every possible scenario. Morning came too soon, the pale light stirring him from a tangle of blankets. Maria was already up and dressed.

"Time to face the day," she said simply, handing Joe a cup of bitter black coffee. He sat up and gratefully accepted it. No matter what uncertainties lay ahead, Joe drew comfort from having Maria steady at his side.

Sam and Jake were geared up and ready to go at first light. Joe saw them off with a clasp of their hands. "Be safe out there. And trust your instincts."

CHAPTER FORTY EIGHT
A GHOST FROM THE PAST

As night fell over the cabin, Joe kept watch on the porch, rifle resting across his knees, waiting for the return of Sam and Jake. Hopeful that they may be able to make new allies in this new sick and twisted world they find themselves in. He breathed in the crisp country air, grateful to have his family together under one roof.

Inside, laughter rang out as Jojo entertained the group with funny stories from his army days.

In the kitchen, Maria and Taylor bonded like old friends as they washed up dinner dishes. Parker dozed in Toni's lap by the fire, the elder woman gently stroking her curly hair.

Curled up on the sofa reading, Claire kept stealing glances at Jojo across the room, Abby sitting unnaturally close to him. Catching her eye, Jojo held her gaze for a moment then gave her a little wink. Claire blushed and quickly looked back down at her book.

For all the troubles still facing them in this uncertain new world, tonight was a rare moment of peace and community that filled Joe's heart to overflowing. Against all odds, they had made it here, and together this family would get through anything the future held.

Maria joined Joe on the porch, snuggling up next to him, with her head on his shoulder. "Joe, it's so peaceful here and now, it's hard to believe all around us the world is falling apart."

Joe reflecting on his past said, "I can still remember bringing the kids here so many times as they were growing up. It was such an escape from our life in Miami. Everyone here was always so nice. Being right on the lake, we would take the boat out and fish all day. That's one of the reasons I chose this place by the way, I figured if the worst ever did happen, at least we could feed ourselves by fishing. There are plenty of fish out there and there are all sorts of game around here as well, Deer, turkey, ducks, geese, all kinds of game in these parts. Not to mention gators!

Maria jolted up, "Gators?"

"Oh yeah." Joe said, "I guess I should warn you, don't go swimming in the lake." he said laughing. "There are gators in there."

Maria sank back onto his shoulder saying, "Well, I guess that's good to know."

Joe looked at Maria with a big grin, "Gators are good eatin' sweetie. I have to admit, when we were out fishing on Lake Harris, I always made it a point to motor over to the Hideaway and get some Gator Bites, man their Gator Bites were the most tender I've ever had, So Good."

Maria, confused, asked, "The Hideaway, What's the Hideaway?"

Joe started stroking Maria's hair feeling how soft it was and enjoying this private moment reflecting on better times with his kids, "Oh the Hideaway is on the east side of the lake, it's kind of a biker bar, but everyone is welcome there and it's...no, it was... such a chill atmosphere. We used to pull up the boat, tie it to the dock, and go grab some great grub. We always had to get the Gator Bites and I might have downed my fair share of whiskey sours while I was there, damn good times. Sometimes they had a band, and it was just so relaxing. I can't believe you lived not that far away, and you never went there."

Maria, bringing Joe back to the present said, "I wish it was still that way my love, I would love to share that experience with you, but I fear everything has changed now."

Joe agreed, "Yeah, it is hard to believe that less than ten miles or so away from where we sit, all hell is breaking loose in a wild west town. Run by some maniac, actually branding women and selling favors."

Maria jokingly says, "Has anything really changed from the old world, Joe? The only thing that has changed are the actors."

Joe says, "Actually you make a good point, when you put it that way, nothing has really changed but the people involved. I guess it's just human nature."

Maria snuggles closer and says, "Well, not everyone's human nature, certainly not your nature, not my nature. Just some sick people's nature. Finding an opening and exploiting it for their own gain. What kind of man can take advantage like that?"

Joe pulls her closer and says, "There are all kinds of sick minds out there sweetie, who knows what drives people to enslave others and gather power for themselves. There have certainly been plenty of them throughout history."

Joe listed, "Hitler, Stalin, Mussolini, Pol Pot, Franco, Pinochet and I guess you can now add the name Warner."

Maria rose from Joe's shoulder, "The name what?"

Joe looked at her surprised, "Warner, Chuck Warner"

Maria stared into Joe's eyes, her face turning ashen, "What?"

Joe, looking puzzled and asked, "What, what?"

Maria sternly said, "The name of the Mayor of New Leesburg is Chuck Warner?"

Joe, confused, said, "Yeah Chuck Warner is the creep in charge of all this misery, why?"

Maria looked sternly at Joe and said, "Joe, Chuck Warner is my husband."

CHAPTER FORTY NINE
SHOCKING REVELATIONS

Joe stared at Maria in stunned silence, her words hitting him like a gut punch. Chuck Warner, the depraved ruler of New Leesburg, was her husband? The man forcing women into sexual slavery was the same man she had been trying to divorce? Joe's mind reeled.

"How...how is this possible?" Joe finally managed; his voice hoarse.

Maria grasped Joe's hands imploringly. "Believe me, I had no idea the monster Chuck had become since I left him. The man I knew was unfaithful and selfish, but not evil."

Joe raked a hand through his hair, shaking his head in disbelief. "Jesus, Maria...if I'd known who he was to you, I never would've..." His voice trailed off as the implications sank in.

"He is not my husband, not in my heart," Maria said vehemently. "That man died the day I walked away. Whoever rules that town now is a stranger to me."

Joe searched Maria's face, seeing only sincerity in her eyes. He let out a heavy sigh. "I believe you didn't know. But this changes things between us."

Maria tightened her grip on Joe's hands. "Please, don't say that. What we have is real." Desperation tinged her voice.

"I just need some time to process this," Joe said heavily. He gently extracted his hands and stood. "Let's pick this up again in the morning."

Maria opened her mouth to protest but thought better of it. She gave a silent nod. Joe touched her shoulder briefly, then turned and headed inside, his footsteps echoing hollowly on the wooden floor.

Alone on the darkened porch, Maria buried her face in her hands as tears streamed down her cheeks. Just when she had allowed herself to feel hope again, her cruel past had found a way to tear it all down. She only prayed Joe would find a way to forgive her tangled history once the shock wore off.

But deep down, a dark fear gnawed at Maria - that this revelation had shattered the trust between them for good. Chuck had already taken so much from her. She couldn't bear it if he stole her future with Joe as well. Overwhelmed by despair, Maria wept bitterly into the night.

CHAPTER FIFTY
HEARTACHE AND HOPE

Morning's pale light filtered into the bedroom, rousing Joe from a fitful sleep. The empty space beside him in bed startled him for a moment before the previous night came crashing back.

Throwing on clothes, Joe hurried from the room. His gut churned with unease not knowing where Maria had gone.

He found her sitting alone at the kitchen table, hands wrapped around a mug of coffee. She started at his sudden entrance.

"Maria," Joe exhaled in relief.

She stood quickly, fresh tears springing to her eyes. "Joe..." she began tremulously.

He crossed the room in two quick strides and enveloped her in his embrace. "I'm sorry about last night," he murmured into her hair. "It was a shock for sure, but we'll get through this."

Maria clung to him, overcome with emotion. When she finally found her voice, she said "You have to believe me Joe, I never knew how sick Chuck was inside, I saw many of his flaws and that's why I've been trying to divorce him for the last few years. Joe, I despise the man Chuck has become."

Joe brushed a stray hair back from her face. "I know, I know sweetie. What matters is the woman you are now." He brought his lips to hers in a fierce, desperate kiss.

When they finally broke apart, breathless, Joe rested his forehead against Maria's. "I can't lose you," he whispered.

"You won't," Maria promised.

Their tender moment was shattered by the sound of the front door banging open. Jake and Sam entered, followed by a ragtag group of strangers.

Joe released Maria and turned to the new arrivals in surprise. "You're back. And I see you brought company."

Jake nodded. "Refugees from Leesburg. They need help." His tone brooked no argument.

"Of course," Joe replied. He studied the hollow, haunted faces looking back at him and felt only compassion. "You're safe now. Come on, let's get you fed and rested."

As the newcomers settled in, Jake and Sam filled Joe in on all they had learned about Chuck's operation in Leesburg. The intel was invaluable, painting a clearer picture of the misery Maria's husband had wrought on the townspeople. Joe felt his anger towards Chuck growing.

"We'll figure out our next steps tomorrow," Joe told them. "For now, let's make our guests feel at home."

While the others tended to the refugees, Joe pulled Maria aside. "This changes nothing between us," he said firmly. "We're in this together."

Maria smiled in gratitude, but Joe noticed it didn't reach her eyes. A shadow remained there of determination, or resignation. The meaning eluded him, but he was too tired to press further.

As they retired to bed, Joe felt Maria cling to him tighter than usual. He attributed it to their emotional reconciliation and soon drifted off with her head tucked under his chin.

CHAPTER FIFTY ONE
HEARTBREAK AND RAGE

Morning sun streamed through the curtains, rousing Joe from sleep. He reached across the bed, finding the space next to him cold and empty. Bolting upright, he saw Maria's belongings were gone.

Racing downstairs in a panic, he spotted a folded piece of paper on the counter with his name on it. With dread, he lifted the note in Maria's graceful script:

"My dearest Joe,

By the time you read this, I will be gone. I am so sorry for leaving without discussing it with you first. I know you will be angry with me and deeply hurt, but please try to understand - confronting Chuck is something I must do alone.

I can't begin to express my sorrow and shame over the atrocities Chuck has committed. To think the man, I once loved could be responsible for such evil horrifies me. Everything I knew has been turned upside down.

In the short time we've known each other, I've come to care for you more deeply than I ever thought possible, especially after the heartbreak of my failed marriage. You showed me that true love still exists in this world. Every moment we've shared has been precious to me. I will always carry the memories of our time together in my heart.

Which is why I need you to know that leaving was agonizing. But finding out the man responsible for so much suffering is my own husband...I can't ignore that. There is too much history and too many unresolved feelings. I have to face Chuck myself and appeal to any shred of goodness left in him. I know him better than anyone. Perhaps I am the only one who stands a chance of reaching what's left of his humanity.

I realize it's dangerous and you'll be angry with me. But this is my burden to bear. All I can do is pray that we'll be reunited when it's over. My only wish is to help end this nightmare, then return to your arms where I belong.

No matter how this ends, please remember one thing - you gave me hope again when I had lost everything. My heart is forever yours. I love you,

Joseph Kelly. Wait for me.

Yours always,

Maria"

Joe's hands trembled, his eyes burning with tears. That brave, stubborn, beautiful woman. She had sacrificed everything for the slim chance of redeeming a monster.

Anger and devastation warred within Joe. He should never have let her slip away. But it wasn't too late. He would bring her back or die trying.

Jaw set, Joe strode outside where Jojo and the others were conversing around the campfire. They turned to him in surprise.

"Get your weapons and gear," Joe barked. "We're going after Maria."

AFTERWORD

I want to thank you once again for taking the time to read this book, and I truly hope I was able to entertain you for a bit.

It is a series, so there is definitely more to come.

I wanted to let everyone know, I did have all my family members read this book before publication to get their feedback.

They all seemed to enjoy it. Hell, why wouldn't they? They all went from their humdrum everyday lives to people who are doing incredible things to survive within these pages.

Finally, the best response actually came from my ex-wife. We are actually still friends, although I was a bit nervous about her reaction to me having her sexually assaulted in this story. I feared she, not to mention my kids, might not react so well to that little plot twist.

I am glad to report my ex took it in stride. After reading the book, she said she very much enjoyed it.

She did have one comment on that assault scene which is a tribute to her good nature. In a text to me she simply asked.

"I couldn't have found that tire iron a few minutes earlier? LOL."

I must take this opportunity to thank her for being such a good sport. She really did make me laugh out loud after reading that text. So, thank you for that Paulette.

Again, I hope you enjoyed this and stay tuned, there is more to come.

Bruno Brennan

Your review on Amazon means so much and is greatly appreciated. You can scan the QR code below to leave a review to help others with your thoughts. Thank you so much in advance.

SIGN UP FOR MY NEWSLETTER

Be the first to know about new book releases, see behind the scenes content and more.

BrunoBrennan.com

www.ingramcontent.com/pod-product-compliance
Lightning Source LLC
Chambersburg PA
CBHW030937260626
47169CB00002B/518